NORTH SEA HUNTERS

BRAD HARMER-BARNES

SEVERED PRESS
HOBART TASMANIA

NORTH SEA HUNTERS

Copyright © 2017 Brad Harmer-Barnes
Copyright © 2017 by Severed Press

WWW.SEVEREDPRESS.COM

ISBN: 978-1-925597-85-1

*To Charlie, for encouraging me to do this, and
Rey, for giving me a reason to.*

At the start of the Second World War in September of 1939, the German Kriegsmarine was in possession of forty-six operational U-Boats.

A U-Boat commander's primary mission was to operate against merchant ships, with the intent to cut off supplies to Great Britain. By the end of 1939, one hundred and fourteen merchant ships had been sunk by U-Boats.

The U-Boats were not invulnerable, however, and one in five U-Boats and their crews had also been lost. While excellent at hiding and striking from underwater, submarines were extremely susceptible to depth charges, and bombing or strafing runs from aeroplanes.

Then there is the case of the U-Boat known only as "U-616".

Names of personnel and ships have been changed, as requested by their nation's respective governments.

"The only thing that ever really frightened me during the war was the U-Boat peril."

-        *Winston Churchill*

-ONE-

"Alarm!"

The men who had – until now – been relaxing atop the deck of U-616 practically fell down the ladder into the darkened control room, in their haste to fulfil their allocated task. Bells rang and klaxons sounded as the crew of the Type VIIB U-Boat quickly began preparations to submerge. The crew span cranks, yanked levers and fastened bulkheads as the ballast tanks of the submarine began to fill with the sea water that would give them the necessary weight to sink below the waves.

Kapitänleutnant August Krauser had been in command of the U-616 ever since the war had started, though of his crew of forty-four, only twenty or so of the original members remained. Some had died in action, of course, but some had been transferred to other boats, or since promoted to command of their own vessels. They had been replaced by fresh, new faces, some of whom seemed barely old enough to grow a beard during the course of the two week long patrol. Nevertheless, regardless of their individual experience levels, the crew around him worked in unison, adjusting the levers and controls necessary for the boat to dive.

Krauser swept his gaze across the control room, where his second-in-command, Johann Hertz, was already in position. Slightly below average height, Hertz ran a hand through his dark blonde hair and flashed a smile to the captain, the grime and sweat on his face causing Krauser's stomach to turn. *Of course*, he thought to himself, absently rubbing at the week's-worth of growth on his face, *you're looking no better.* Appearances were of no importance while at sea.

"Well, gentlemen...what do we have?" he asked, approaching the periscope.

"It's a freighter," replied Kleiner, his chief engineer. "We only just spotted it on the horizon when we called the alarm; but I'd hazard a guess that it's four – perhaps even five – thousand tonnes."

Krauser tried his best not to let his surprise (and perhaps a little excitement) show on his face. Kleiner had served with the U-616 since the beginning, and it was not uncommon for the man to get a little excitable as "The Hunt" approached. "Five thousand tonnes would be rather a large target, and a large victory for us."

"Yes, sir."

"Hertz, periscope."

Hertz span down the periscope, and moved it into the correct position, before standing aside to offer control to the captain.

Krauser peered through the lenses. It took him a couple of minutes to find Kleiner's freighter.

Attempting to spot a small grey spot against a grey-blue sky and a blue-grey sea was hard enough without the distraction of the waves lapping against the upper lens of the periscope. After a little panning back and forth, he managed to focus on what Kleiner had seen. It was indeed a freighter; there was no mistaking that. The engineer had somewhat overestimated its size, but it was at least three thousand tonnes. Not exactly the trophy he had been secretly hoping for, but still a worthwhile target.

"Slow down," he said. "Let's keep low and attempt to engage when it turns dark. I can't make out if it has an escort, and I don't want to run the risk of coming across a destroyer in full daylight."

"Yes, sir." said Hertz.

"It doesn't seem to be travelling very fast, so I think we can keep it in sight until then. What do you think, Mr Hertz?"

"I agree, sir."

Krauser suppressed a sigh. "But you have another suggestion, don't you?"

His second in command feigned confusion. "Sir?"

Krauser straightened up and raised an eyebrow. At thirty, he was at least five years younger than Hertz, and he knew that this bothered the man. Although, in theory, rank and experience counted for everything; he knew that in actuality men still judged age to be a factor. You were taught from a young age to respect your elders, but respecting a younger man in a higher position than you was hard. "I know you well enough to know that you have an alternative suggestion. I would like to hear it."

Hertz swallowed, before replying. "Sir, the torpedoes are unreliable at best. I'd estimate there's possibly as high as a one in four failure rate. I would prefer to rely on the deck gun, if possible."

Klauser gave the idea some consideration. There was an eighty-eight millimetre cannon mounted to the deck of the boat, but he was sceptical of its uses. You needed to be close and – perhaps more significantly – you needed to be surfaced. The deck gun may be less susceptible to dud rounds than the electric or even steam driven torpedoes, but it was nowhere near as explosive when it did strike a target.

"We will approach the ship as per my orders. Once we are closer, I will reassess the risk and consider using the deck gun. I hope this is satisfactory to you, Mr Hertz?"

"Your orders, sir."

Krauser turned from the command room, and toward the rear of the boat, squeezing past shifting, stinking sailors in the painfully cramped corridor. Food and supplies were stuffed into every nook and cranny in a desperate attempt to save on space. When they had first set out, one of the toilets had been turned into a larder, and wasn't usable until the crew had managed to eat their way through it.

Finally squeezing between a semi-naked gunner and a crate of cured ham, he reached his bunk. Most of the crew had to share a bed. When your shift was finished, you threw out the man sleeping in your allocated space, and replaced him until, several hours later, it was once again his turn to replace you. Being Captain had certain privileges, though, and a bunk of his own was the one that he took the greatest pleasure in. Far from being an opulent, wood panelled cabin, such as he might have been given on a surface ship, it was a bunk like any other on board the boat. It did have two luxuries, however. Firstly, there was a curtain that he could draw for a little privacy. Secondly, he didn't have to share it with anyone. It was his and his alone.

The U-616 was a Type VIIB class U-Boat. Active since 1936, the Type VIIs were the backbone of the German navy – the Kriegsmarine. They were attack boats built to withstand depths of up to two hundred and fifty metres, and had – so far – been the most successful submarines of the war. A capacity of fourteen torpedoes, complemented by Hertz's much loved eighty-eight millimetre deck gun and an anti-aircraft gun placed it head and shoulders above its predecessor, the Type VIIA.

It was obvious to all that even Winston Churchill was rattled by how successful their raids on the North Atlantic and North Sea around the British Mainland had been. Several thousand tonnes of supplies – both civilian and military – had been lost to the "wolfpacks" of submarines operating in unison, or even to lone hunters, such as the position in which the U-616 was now operating.

Krauser opted to leave the curtain to his bunk open. It was nice to have privacy, but it also helped morale if he could show himself to be approachable; and it was only a matter of minutes before someone did stop to see him.

"How are things, my Captain?"

Krauser set down the book that he had yet to make it past page twenty of, and smiled at his old friend.

"Until now, things have been rather too quiet."

Dr Josef Arnold was the ship's medical officer, responsible for taking care of any sick and injured crew. On a good trip, there was nothing for him to do, other than to pitch in during times of great strain and difficulty. A bad trip - such as the previous patrol, which had seen an ensign break both arms when a torpedo tore loose of its mountings - would end in the doctor tired beyond all measure.

"Too quiet? Can there really be such a thing?" asked the doctor.

"Yes, doctor and all too easily. A quiet ship is a quiet crew, and a quiet crew is a bored crew. You know that some of the men have arranged a chess tournament?"

"I'm confident I'll make it through to the quarter finals, at least."

Krauser laughed. "I don't doubt it. Blumenfeld is a good player, though. I think he will take the prize."

"And what is the prize?"

"A bottle and a woman of your choice at the next shore leave."

"Then I expect you shall be playing your hardest?"

The Captain shook his head and sat up in his bunk. "No, I will not be entering. It's uncomfortable for the crew when I join in these things. They don't want to beat me, but they don't want to be seen to be losing too easily to me either. It is better I do not join in."

"It sounds to me like you're trying to avoid losing."

Krauser threw up his hands in defeat. "Yes, yes; I am awful at chess. I lack the ability to plan forward more than one move at a time. Sometimes I can see two, I suppose, but a truly great chess player can be ten, fifteen, twenty moves beyond you, in his head. I lack that foresight, that memory, that…forethought."

Dr Arnold raised his eyebrows. "Rather an odd admission for the captain of a sea vessel, in time of war."

Krauser lowered his voice, now wishing that he did have a cabin or an office of his own. "I suppose that is why this particular role suits me so well. I can cruise along, and only have to come up with a strategy once we actually engage the target. I don't have to worry about where the enemy is three weeks in advance, or the counterintelligence he has. I just have to turn up, and engage on the fly, almost. I will never be a Dönitz, or a Rommel – or even a Churchill, for that matter – but this? This is a job I *can* do."

"I understand completely. For me, every patient is a surprise. I don't know what sickness or injury will greet me until I see it with my own eyes. It is both a blessing and curse."

Krauser stood from his bunk, and gripped the doctor's arm. "It is good, then, that we have both found careers that so suit our abilities and foibles."

The doctor nodded. "Is there anything I can do to help you at present, my Captain?"

Krauser shook his head. "I, and all my chief staff, are well. So, unless you want to provide me some chess lessons…"

"And give away all my best strategies? The prize is mine, sir!"

They were interrupted by the arrival of Hertz, stinking and sweating. "Sir, we have determined that the freighter is unescorted. Permission to surface?"

Krauser nodded. While known for operating underwater, truth be told, U-Boats were only supposed to do so when threatened, or otherwise attempting to avoid detection. "Permission granted. Surface, but slowly if possible."

"Yes, sir." Hertz snapped and headed quickly to the control room.

"He likes being in the control room when you're not there," said Dr Arnold, wryly. "It gives him a chance to play act as captain for a while."

Krauser knew the doctor was right, and it irked him a little. He thought he was the only one who had detected Hertz's suppressed resentment, but apparently this was not the case. "He's a good man. He would make an excellent captain – on another ship, mind – if he managed to get that chip off his shoulder."

"Agreed. Anyway, I shall let you rest. I have chess to practice."

The U-616 sailed slowly through the North Sea, unseen by the Norwegian supply ship *Freyr*, bound for Britain, with a cargo of meat, fish and clothing. An experienced sailor can easily navigate by the moon and the stars, of course; and the crews of both the U-616 and the *Freyr* were experienced, trained and able to do so. Truth be told, most could navigate to their destination armed only with a map and a compass; but the night holds other dangers. Darkness holds other dangers.

The sea is dark, and the sea is deep, and it holds many secrets.

At ten o'clock that night, Krauser climbed from his bunk and made his way to the control room. The attack would begin shortly.

-TWO-

Krauser stepped into the control room to salutes from Hertz and the attendant seamen. There was a tension in the air, such as always preceded an attack like this. Days and days of no action took a toll on the men who had signed up to do their part for their country, and nothing blew off some steam quite like firing a brace of torpedoes towards a fat, juicy target.

"Report, Mr Hertz," said Krauser, stepping to the periscope.

"Vessel is a Norwegian freighter, sir. Heading for either North England or Scotland. We're matching speed at fifteen knots, at present. No sign of escort, or air support."

Krauser peered through the periscope at the darkness all around them. The ship was close now, but he was confident that the U-Boat would sit too low in the water to be easily spotted. He was able to read the name *Freyr* on the side. The Norse goddess of the harvest. "Let's go up top. I can't see much through the scope at night."

"Yes, sir."

The two of them, accompanied by four men – two to arm the flak gun, two to the deck gun – climbed up through the hatch. The noise inside a U-Boat was a constant drone of diesel and machinery that was cacophonous at first, but eventually became such a constant background that one barely noticed it. Up top, the waves and the wind were just as loud, but they were jarringly different. The whirring and oscillating of the noises of the U-Boat were at least a constant. The noises of the waves playing against the side of the boat, the howling of the wind, and the distant chug of the *Freyr*'s engines were all somehow discordant and chaotic compared to the consistency of the submarine.

Krauser wished he'd brought a windbreaker up with him, and suppressed a shiver in the North Sea breeze. Hertz had come prepared, and while he said nothing, Krauser still felt as though he was taking this as yet another of his silent victories over the younger captain. He pulled his binoculars up, and studied the vessel. "That hull looks to be reinforced."

"Sir?"

"I don't think the deck gun will penetrate. Prepare to fire torpedoes."

"Sir, I must protest. The deck gun carries eighty-eight millimetre shells; that's more than even our largest tanks can fire, and this is just a freighter…"

"It's a large freighter, Mr Hertz. And I intend to see it destroyed as quickly and efficiently as possible. The torpedoes will not have to worry as much about penetrating the armour, and the wind…The wind, Mr Hertz, will make the deck gun inaccurate. We will fire torpedoes."

"Sir, I really have confidence in our men and our equip-"

"Do you not also have faith in your Captain, Mr Hertz?"

The seamen accompanying them shifted awkwardly in the silence. Krauser mentally cursed. He hated that this showdown had happened in front of the men, regardless of their number. He didn't need rumours of a rift between officers spreading across his boat.

Hertz blinked and composed himself before replying. "I have faith in my Captain, sir."

"See that you do. I have faith in my men, and I have faith in my equipment. All I ask is that they have faith in me in return."

"Yes, sir."

Krauser eyed Hertz for a little longer, before climbing back down into the command room. "Prepare to fire a volley of three steam torpedoes."

The U-616 carried two different types of torpedoes in its arsenal. The G7a was steam propelled, and was by far more reliable and had a greater range than the G7e. The G7e was propelled with the aid of a lead-acid battery, and while it was more susceptible to failure than its steam driven cousin, the lack of jet or tell-tale bubbles made it much harder to detect when fired. However, with no escort on hand to interfere, Krauser felt that the steam driven torpedoes would make a much better option.

Shouts and alarms and knocks and bells indicated that his order was being relayed to the men working the torpedo bay. This was their first attack of this patrol, and the men were ready and eager. The rattles and clanks and gentle groans and screeches rattled around the ship, and back to the command room as the seven metre long torpedoes were slid into their compartments, and the bulkheads sealed shut behind them.

Krauser peered through the periscope one more time. This moment was the one he hated and loved the most. The moment where he could feel the present being split into two different futures, one where he called off the attack, and was not responsible for the deaths of innocent people; and the one he knew that he had to take, where the war marched on, and his part was but a minor speck of ash in the fire that consumed the world.

The moment seemed to drag until he finally broke the oppressive silence. "Fire one."

Shouts of "Fire One!" echoed down the noisy, humid length of the boat as his order was relayed once more. Then there was a shuddering jolt felt the length of the command room as the first torpedo spat forth towards its target.

"First torpedo away, sir!" called Hertz, sweat pouring off his forehead.

Krauser continued to watch through the periscope. The seconds ticked by.

There was no sign of any impact.

The *Freyr* could be no more than three quarters of a kilometre away. That meant that the torpedo should have impacted in – he quickly did the maths – forty-five, fifty seconds, maybe? "Time since launch?" he asked.

"Twenty three seconds, sir," said one of the crew. Krauser nodded his thanks and continued to watch through the periscope.

Forty…forty-five…fifty…

"Any moment now…" the crewman added.

Fifty-five…sixty…sixty five…seventy…

"Dud round," said Krauser, cursing under his breath. The steam driven torpedoes *were* more reliable than the electric ones, but not by much. He didn't know the official figures, but going on personal experience, he estimated that as high as one in two torpedoes could be a dead duck. It was a frustrating and dangerous way to attack an enemy vessel, and it was why he had learned to fire his torpedoes in braces of three.

"Torpedo tubes two and three are locked and loaded, sir," came Hertz's voice. Krauser didn't take his eyes from the viewfinder. When the torpedo hit, he wanted to see the damage it did. Fighting blind was not satisfying. "Fire Two."

Again the echoing of his order, firing like synapses down the length of the U-Boat. Orders relayed, preparations made, controls operated until, finally, the torpedo slid forth from the submarine. The shudder, again, reverberated through the command room. Hertz actually wobbled on his feet a little, reaching out to grab a nearby strut for support. Krauser barely noticed anything, all his concentration focused on the periscope, as he counted again under his breath. Forty-five...fifty...

"They can't both be duds, surely?" whispered Hertz.

A couple of the crew whispered among themselves, but Krauser remained silent. Sixty...sixty five...nothing.

"Someone run down to the engine room," he said. "See if there's a problem."

A crewman turned and left. The control room had gone deathly silent, except for the gentle chugging of the diesel engines. Krauser could feel his jaw aching from the clenching of his teeth. He refused to let himself relax, his discomfort serving to fuel his frustration and anger. Hertz stepped up beside him and made as if to speak, but was cut off.

"Hertz, if you mention that deck gun, I shall fire you out of a torpedo tube myself. We're much too far away to make the range needed, and the wind is still far too strong. If this last torpedo does not do the job, we call off the hunt. I won't keep wasting ammunition like this."

The clanging of footsteps on the grating heralded the return of the crewman, who squeezed his way into the control room again. "Captain, all is running smoothly in the forward tubes. The gunners and loaders can only surmise that both were either dud rounds, or failed to make the range."

Krauser grimaced. "Move us closer."

The submarine shuddered again as the diesel engines revved up, spinning the rear propeller, speeding the U-616 in pursuit of its target. Krauser once again rattled off some mental arithmetic, calculating the estimated distance to the *Freyr* and the speed he guessed they were going, finally calling a halt when he reckoned them to be five-hundred metres from the target. Looking into the periscope again, the magnification allowed him to see people moving around on the deck of the large freighter. Definitely not military. Attacking civilian targets wasn't exactly satisfying, but it was safer. They were far less likely to be able to radio in for air support than a military vessel. Much less likely to return fire, too.

Krauser studied the ship through the periscope, then ordered "Fire three!".

The torpedo shot smoothly from the submarine and powered through the water, leaving a jet of bubbles behind it as the steam propulsion did its work. Krauser counted again, out loud this time. "Twenty…twenty five…"

The *Freyr* visibly lurched to starboard as the torpedo hit its mark. The crew on deck panicked and grabbed for whatever handholds they could reach as the ship rocked sharply to the side under the impact.

"Target hit!" cried Krauser, eliciting a cheer from some of the crew, and a sigh of relief from Hertz. He headed straight for the hatch up top to get a better look at the damage. This was hardly standard operating procedure, but after the tension and the problems with the first two torpedoes, he was desperate to get a better look at U-616's handiwork. Hertz and Kleiner followed up shortly afterwards.

The *Freyr* was still visibly rocking from the impact. Strangely, though, no smoke or fire was immediately apparent. The warheads of the torpedoes carried a hefty wallop behind them – they had to, for penetrating a ship's hull was no small feat – and they frequently caught the ammunition or fuel aboard their target, resulting in large flames and smoke clouds that could hang over the area for days. Krauser squinted through the salt spray and tried to get a better look at the damage he had wrought.

Hertz studied through a pair of binoculars. "They're abandoning ship, sir."

Krauser held out his hand and Hertz handed the binoculars to him. He focused on the life boats, and was surprised to see that Hertz was right. "We must have really hit them good, if they're already abandoning their ship and cargo…"

"Maybe they're carrying something volatile? Fuel, or chemicals, perhaps? If a shipment like that were to go up, it wouldn't leave a man jack of the crew alive to tell the tale."

"I don't know so much. You would think that they'd at least spend some time attempting repairs, or to…I don't know. I mean, it'd take some serious damage before I gave the order to abandon our boat."

"We don't have the luxury of life boats, sir."

"You know what I mean," Krauser snapped, "These men are panicked beyond what you would expect. Do you think maybe one of the earlier torpedoes did hit, without us noticing?"

Hertz rubbed his straggly beard; shaving was forbidden while at sea, as a waste of water. "Unlikely, sir. We noticed that impact straight away, and the G7a torpedoes are a little…how can I put this…inconsistent?"

"You'll get no argument from me on that matter, Mr Hertz. In any event, this ship is as good as sunk. Tell the men of our victory, and let's get underway."

Krauser was climbing back down the ladder to the control room, when Kleiner's voice stopped him. "Sir? There's something…strange, sir."

Krauser looked over. He had once again forgotten his windbreaker, and didn't appreciate the delay in getting back down in the warmth of the control room. However, Kleiner was not a man who was easily rattled, and his vision was second to none on board.

"The lifeboats, sir."

"What of them?"

"They're…they're sinking, sir."

-THREE-

Krauser didn't quite know how to react to this news. He hesitated, half in and half out of the conning tower. "Sinking?"

Kleiner raised his binoculars back to his eyes and turned to the rapidly sinking *Freyr*. "Yes, sir...there goes one...my god!"

Krauser clambered back up onto the deck, barging past Hertz and snatching the binoculars from Kleiner, the poor chief engineer nearly choking as the strap was pulled against his neck. He swept his gaze across the length of the Norwegian freighter. The crew was still running back and forth in a panic, like ants whose nest has been kicked, scrabbling back and forth to protect their Queen and repair the damage as quickly as possible. Arms waved, and he could almost imagine that he heard the shouts and calls of the crew, though he was too far out to hear anything beyond a general cacophony.

He watched through the darkness as a lifeboat, loaded up with fifteen, perhaps twenty men, was lowered jerkily into the foaming sea. The small crew desperately tried to distribute their weight and settle supplies comfortably, then set to rowing, fleeing the sinking freighter.

"It just...disappeared," muttered Kleiner, next to him.

Krauser shushed him, and continued to observe the sinking ship. There were now five lifeboats dispersed about a hundred metres out from the listing hull of the *Freyr* - some of the men panicked, others eerily calm. One boat, the nearest the stern of the freighter, was much more excitable. The men were all standing and pointing to a spot on the sea fifty or sixty yards from them. The crew were almost jumping up and down in their excitement. Had they perhaps spotted some supplies that were bobbing in the water? Or had one of their number fallen overboard and was in desperate need of assistance?

Hertz called him from near the entrance hatch, causing him to look away for a moment. "Sir, we need to move. The crew of the freighter may have already called for assistance. The Navy or the RAF could already be on their way, and we need to be long gone when they arrive."

Krauser waved him away. "Head below and prepare to move out, Mr Hertz, but wait for us to return. Mr Kleiner and I will observe a little longer."

Hertz hesitated, before replying coldly. "Your orders, sir."

The dull clanging sounds as his second in command headed back to the control room felt like a physical relief to Krauser. He was beginning to feel increasingly tense whenever the man was around, as if preparing himself for another confrontation like earlier that day, or perhaps even for a physical attack. He made a mental note to suggest Hertz for promotion to another boat when he finished this patrol. Life was tough enough at sea without extra challenges.

Krauser looked back across the sea at the *Freyr*, the night time darkness that had aided their initial attack now becoming a hindrance as he tried to trace the movement of the lifeboats across the dark water. He again found the spot that the crew of the last boat had been pointing to, and tried to focus on what they had found. There, something flashed in the darkness, a little particle of white in a pot of black ink. The waves swelled again, obscuring his vision for a moment before the whiteness flashed again. He adjusted the focus and held his breath to steady his movements a little.

A white piece of driftwood bobbed up and down in the water, then another. The wood looked as though it had been shattered at one side, the jagged edge spinning this way and that in the water.

He panned quickly back to the nearest lifeboat. The crew were still pointing excitedly, some seeming to be shouting, while those at the oars rapidly rowed away from the driftwood. Krasuer felt the hairs on his arms rise as realisation dawned. The boats were the same colour and material as the gently spinning debris.

A scream echoed across the water towards them, and he quickly span to what he assumed to be the source. A large wake spread in between two of the other lifeboats…but one of them was gone! Rocked up and down in the large waves spreading from the centre of the wake, the men, like the crew of the other boat, started panicking and screaming.

"Did you see that?" asked Kleiner.

"Could they have been carrying explosives, or something like that? Not sea mines, but maybe Mills Bombs, or landmines? Perhaps the cargo broke loose and two of the lifeboats were unfortunate enough to bump into them?"

"No, sir…that last one…Hell, sir…it went straight down. There was no explosion, nothing like that. It just…sank. Down."

"Then what the hell could cause that? A structural fault with the boat?"

Krauser trained the binoculars back on the new spot. White planks of wood surfaced…and then the chilling sight of a man, face down, his orange life jacket making him stand out in the darkness.

Kleiner managed to slip his neck out of the binocular strap and stand upright. "I don't know, sir. Maybe…but with two of the boats?"

"A defective batch, maybe?"

He returned his gaze to the floating man in the water. He knew he had to be dead, but one of the lifeboats was rowing toward him, a man at the prow extending a billhook to try and fish the sailor from the water. It took a couple of tentative jabs – the billhooks were hardly precision instruments – but the sailor finally managed to catch a hold of the man's lifejacket. Two more of the crew came to his aid in hefting him from the water, but the lone man could probably have done it himself.

The darkness and the moonlight made the sight of the man's torso - raggedly cut off at the waist, the one remaining arm trailing in the water - even more ghoulish than it would have been in broad daylight. As one, the crew of the lifeboat screamed, the leader dropping the billhook in the water, and the men at the oars chaotically rowing away from the grisly scene.

"What the hell?" cried Krauser, dropping the binoculars to the deck.

"That's no landmine, no mechanical failure..." gasped Kleiner. "That's a shark attack."

"A shark can't sink a lifeboat!" shouted Krauser, heading for the entrance hatch.

"I saw one do it myself, sir. I was stationed in the Pacific and I saw one smash straight through the hull of a fishing boat."

"Did the boat sink?"

"Eventually, sir. The crew were all rescued, but it was scary as hell for all the men on board."

"These lifeboats are not sinking slowly enough for that. These ships are just...dropping!"

Another scream carried across the water. Krauser span, and squinted across the darkness. Kleiner grabbed the binoculars, and gasped. "Another one...it's...the...God, the *size* of it!"

Krauser, buffeted by the wind, hurried to the chief engineer and snatched the binoculars, fumbling them as a large wave rocked the U-Boat. He cursed as they bounced off the hull and into the ocean. "What?" he demanded, gripping the rail again "What was it?"

"Shark!" the chief engineer shouted. "I saw the fin as it went below again and...Captain...it must have been two metres high."

A loud booming wave came from the direction of the freighter, and Krauser span, expecting to see an explosion bursting from the hull of the *Freyr*, but instead all he saw was a massive spray of foam near where one of the lifeboats had been. Only one now remained, the men inside screaming as they rode the tumultuous wave of foam, driftwood and blood that swelled under, around and over them. From the ambient lighting of the rapidly sinking freighter, he saw the shadow of a fin, easily two metres high, glide through the water. What the hell could be so large?

He'd seen Great White sharks swimming two or three times when stationed in the Atlantic, and their fins could only have been half a metre high. A three metre dorsal fin just...wasn't possible. Maybe the light and shadow from the sinking ship had thrown out his vision, the swell and movement of the water making the size impossible to judge accurately. Perhaps it could even be something else. An experimental submarine operating in these waters that he hadn't been informed about.

Impossible. In any event, the Kriegsmarine wouldn't launch a submarine whose sole purpose was to destroy lifeboats. There was a war on, but their mission was to sink the cargo and the ships; most captains – himself included – attempted to spare and save as many of the sailors' lives as they could. It helped to alleviate the guilt some of them felt over how clandestine and underhanded submarine warfare was by its very nature.

Also there was the ragged, torn torso that the survivors of the *Freyr* had fished out of the water. No submarine would do that. No submarine *could* do that. An explosion, perhaps. A man dragged into a propeller, maybe. But not a sinking lifeboat.

He had a sick feeling in his stomach as he rushed to the entrance to the control room, bracing his feet on the sides of the ladder and sliding into the red, humid stink of the control room. "Half speed ahead. Those sailors are in serious danger, and I intend to assist them."

"We don't have space to take on fifty survivors, Captain!" snapped Hertz. "Where could we put them? Even one of the toilets is filled up with food supplies. There's simply not the space."

"We don't take them on board, Mr Hertz. I merely said that I intend to assist them. Three of those life boats have been sunk by shark attacks already, and I intend to make sure that the last one survives."

"Shark attack? What sort of sharks does one find in the North Sea, Captain?"

Kleiner had followed them down and cocked an eye contemptuously at the second in command.

"Angel Sharks, Blue Sharks, Thresher Sharks, Catsharks, Basking Sharks…"

Krauser suppressed a smile at seeing Hertz sufficiently berated. "Plus whatever that is out there. It's big enough to sink three lifeboats so far. Could be a Great White. Perhaps they come here sometimes."

"It's possible," shrugged Kleiner, "but that thing looked far too big to be a Great White to me, sir."

Krauser nodded acknowledgment as he felt the engines kick in, powering the U-Boat towards the last lifeboat. "Let's get some men up top ready to provide assistance if needed. Small firearms at the ready, in case our Norwegian friends are feeling a little excitable. I'd like Doctor Arnold informed. He may have some patients very soon. Warn him about the possibility of shark wounds."

"Sir!" snapped Hertz and rushed off to inform the doctor.

Krauser estimated they could be on top of the lifeboat in as few as five minutes, and he intended to be ready to provide assistance - personally if need be. He ran to his bunk, grabbed, checked and loaded his Mauser pistol, and…for the first time today…managed to stop and grab his windbreaker before heading up the ladder, and onto the deck.

One lifeboat remained, and it was in a sorry state.

-FOUR-

The U-616 was a hive of activity as the submarine rushed to the aid of the last lifeboat. Captain Krauser was already up on the main deck, sprayed with salt and foam. Gripping tightly onto the handrail, he kept his eyes firmly fastened on the last lifeboat. With just a crew of four, the small vessel was thrown around, up and down in the chaotic waters around the sinking *Freyr*. The men inside shouted to each other in Norwegian, their hands tightly gripping the seats, the sides of the boat, the oars – anything they could grab a hold of in order to avoid being hurled into the freezing cold North Sea. The waves splashed up and over the prow, and the men were now ankle deep in the freezing cold water. They had pulled on life jackets, but Krauser knew that they would do little to protect them from either the freezing, black water – or the silent teeth and jaws that hunted them.

Krauser cupped his hands to his mouth and shouted through the wind and clamour that help was coming, hoping they could both hear him and understand German. When they were little more than a hundred metres from the lifeboat, one of its occupants looked up and saw him. Krauser guessed him to be in his early thirties, blonde and bearded. A mixture of relief, fear and resignation washed across his face. The man reached back, slapping a comrade's arm, calling something to attract the rest of the crew. Two of them stopped to look over to the U-Boat and froze. Krauser shouted to his men to slow approach so that the submarine could be boarded easily by the survivors.

The last crew member of the lifeboat, however, did not react to either the shouts of his friend, or to the diesel engine chug of the submarine. His gaze remained fixed at a point in the water a hundred metres away to the stern of the small vessel. Suddenly, his eyes widened, his jaw dropped, and his face paled. Losing his balance, he fell clumsily into the boat, setting it rocking up and down on the waves once more.

The other three sailors staggered, grabbed their seats and shouted at their companion. Unheeding, still he gabbled and gibbered, pointing off to the stern of the boat. The U-616 was only fifty metres away now, and Krauser could just about hear them speaking, though he did not understand their language. The hysterical man's voice was high and shrieking, as the others began gasping and looking in the direction he was gesturing. He turned to see what it was they had spotted, and adrenaline filled his own heart in a cold flush. His first reaction was that the massive, turbulent wake had to be a torpedo. He'd seen often enough the damage that these seven metre long weapons of destruction could wreak. Even if the lifeboat was the target of the attack, the shock wave could easily damage, and possibly even sink a U-616.

The surf above the wave broke, and he felt his knees buckle, forcing him to support himself on the handrail. The shark's fin that smoothly rose through the spray like a knife through butter had to be two and a half, perhaps even three metres tall. That would make the shark itself...thirty metres long. Impossible!

Once, on shore leave, he had seen a Great White that a fisherman had caught and cut open. Even that monster of the sea had only been six metres in length; and all had said that was a large one. As the gargantuan fin sped towards the lifeboat, it slowly submerged again, the wake still speeding to the defenceless Norwegian crew.

"Did you see that?" screamed Kleiner, standing next to him. "It's a monster, sir!"

Krauser suppressed a shiver and swallowed before replying. He had seen it, although he knew he had to be mistaken. "It's still just a shark, Mr Kleiner. Get ready to take those men on board."

He turned back, just in time. The shark collided with the boat, causing it to splintering it into two. With a crash and a stifled scream, the men inside and all their supplies fell into the freezing cold North Sea. There was a momentary call for help, and then all were submerged.

The deck fell silent for a moment. Everyone kept their eyes focused on the spot where the boat had last been seen - some hoping for the men to surface so that a rescue could still be attempted, others hoping for a better glimpse of the colossal shark that had claimed this area of the water as its own.

Krauser scanned the debris. More white driftwood. A first aid kit. A duffel bag. The detritus of a failed escape.

He let the binoculars fall to hang on the strap about his neck. The *Freyr* was halfway sunk by now, and there was no sign of any crew on board, or any lifeboats being evacuated. There was little now that the crew of U-616 could do. They had wrought their destruction on the freighter, and now they had to continue their patrol, on to the next target. "Prepare to move out," he said to Kleiner. "We're done here."

As he turned to head down to the control room, he heard a solitary cry for help. The others on the deck heard it, too. Captain Krauser ran to the prow of the U-Boat's deck and thought he could see someone waving near the debris. Pulling the binoculars up, he hurriedly focused on the spot. It was the blonde man who had first seen them! Somehow he had escaped the carnage that the shark had wrought and was still alive!

"Belay that last order!" Krauser shouted. "There is a survivor. Slow ahead and bring us as close as you can. I will not leave that man to be fish food!"

The diesel engines shuddered into life once more, and the submarine slowly pushed towards the flailing man. His motions were already slowing noticeably from the cold, and Krauser knew that there could only be a short time before he succumbed to the sudden temperature drop.

The man had managed to catch hold of a piece of driftwood, and lay still, hanging from it in the water. Krauser gritted his teeth as the submarine moved closer. They were only thirty metres from him by now. He shouted out to the man. "Hello, down there!"

The man raised his head, but gave no other signal that he had heard, and remained silent.

Krauser tried calling out to the man in English. He knew no Norwegian but was sure he remembered hearing from a fellow captain that most of the Scandinavian countries spoke English as a second language. He had joked that they spoke it even better than the English did, themselves. "Are you able to swim to us? We have food and medical supplies and will arrange for your delivery home, once we return to Germany."

The man nodded, and began to kick his legs in the water, propelling his small piece of driftwood toward the U-616. Kleiner hurried to his captain's side with a length of rope, looped to act as an improvised lifesaver. As the man got within twenty metres of the submarine, Kleiner spun and threw it out to rest in the water.

"We have Roy Rogers on board..." joked Krauser, under his breath. Kleiner gave a wry smile, acknowledging the joke, but still terrified for the man - and of the shark that, for all they knew, still loitered in the area, patrolling its home.

The man reached the lasso, and pulled the heavy, wet rope over his head and slid an arm through, gripping it tightly. Kleiner and another of the men began to reel the survivor aboard. After what seemed like an age, the man – dripping cold, salty water - finally clambered up onto the deck.

Krauser extended a hand. "Welcome aboard the U-616. I am Captain August Krauser, and I wish to offer you our hospitality."

The man shivered and accepted the proffered handshake. "Dahlen. Arild Dahlen."

They were interrupted by a massive metallic collision sound from the direction of the *Freyr*. The two thousand ton freighter was rocking back and forth in the water, sending waves spreading out and in their direction. The submarine was far enough out to avoid being tossed around, but the water still lapped up and over the wooden deck in places. Krauser wondered if the *Freyr* could have been unfortunate enough to have hit a rock, or perhaps even a sea mine, as it sank.

The Norwegian man joined them in staring out over the water. "Captain Krauser, I strongly advise that you get your ship out of this area as fast as you can."

Krauser met his gaze, and something unspoken passed between the two men. "I intend to do just that, Mr Dahlen. Mr Kleiner, I will escort Mr Dahlen to Dr Arnold; please see that we move out as fast as possible."

Krauser guided Dahlen back down the deck to the entrance hatch. "You saw it then?" asked the Norwegian.

"I don't fear sharks, Mr Dahlen. I fear reports of your sinking reaching the British Navy or Air Force, and them launching their own missions to sink us in return."

Dahlen stopped walking and turned to the captain. "What do you mean?"

Krauser grimaced, remembering that he had just killed several of this man's friends. "It was nothing personal on our part, Mr Dahlen, but we are under orders to sink as many cargo vessels bound for Britain as we can. As we are responsible for the torpedo strike which sank your vessel, we can expect retaliation. As such, I intend to be long gone from the area before that happens."

The Norwegian half-smiled to himself, and stepped closer to the captain. Krauser's hand went to his Mauser, lest the man was about to attempt a misguided escape effort.

Dahlen's eyes flickered to the gun, and he stopped, but did not back away. Instead, cocking his head, he whispered. "You think *you* sank the ship?"

-FIVE-

Dahlen's face crumpled with disgust and he suppressed a gag as soon as he reached the bottom of the ladder into the control room. The noxious cocktail of diesel engine fumes, over-ripening food, and the body odour of forty-two unwashed men was something that Krauser had become immune to over the course of the patrol. Their Norwegian captive had no such luxury and it had hit him like a punch to the stomach. The noise, too, must have been jarring to a man who had only ever sailed above the water. Every rattle and hiss of every piston reverberated around the submarine, creating a constant white noise background that was, well, actually comforting, after a fashion - but at first it was monstrous.

Krauser smiled as the dazed man took in his surroundings. "Welcome aboard the U-616, Mr Dahlen."

Dahlen nodded an acknowledgment and, at Krasuer's direction, moved down the central corridor, squeezing past men and baggage, where necessary, and trying to get his head around moving through the hatchways and openings of a U-Boat. Eventually, they reached the bunk of Dr Arnold. The doctor had already been informed of the arrival of their new passenger, and had prepared his examination equipment. He extended his hand and introduced himself.

Dahlen appeared to be nervous and wary, which was understandable. Krauser supposed that the man had probably been hearing about the vicious, barbaric ways of the enemy since the outbreak of the war. He did not take it personally. Demonising the enemy was a psychological tactic that went back possibly even earlier than the days of Hannibal or Alexander the Great, and he had no doubt that some of his men expected the British and Polish fighters to be equally as monstrous. It was simply part of how wars were fought.

Dr Arnold sat the man down on his bunk and began an examination. "How old are you, Mr Dahlen?" he asked in English, checking the man's pupil reaction.

"Thirty two," the man replied, before turning his gaze on Captain Krauser. "I am gracious for your hospitality, Captain; but I regret that it has been a very long day, and I am very tired."

"You can sleep when the doctor is done examining you," replied Krauser. "And I do apologise for the loss of your friends and crewmates. That was one of the most aggressive sharks I have ever seen."

Dahlen laughed, once, derisively. "You are not joking. Captain Krauser, I am not convinced that thing was not the devil himself, sent to punish the crew of the *Freyr* for whatever dark reason known only to itself."

Krauser leant against the wall on the other side of the corridor and folded his arms. "Today wasn't the first time you had seen it, then?"

Dahlen shook his head. "It started following the ship three days ago. At least, that is when we first noticed it. While we were working on deck, Øystein, another crewman, spotted the thing's wake. He was excited at first, as he thought it might be seals or dolphins. He was a simple, young man, not long to the ocean, and such things were still a novelty to him. I remember he grabbed my arm and pulled me over to the boat, keen to show me. I saw no dolphins or seals, however. I did see a giant wake, and then, sliding up through the surf like a bayonet, that thing's monstrous fin.

"I clapped Øystein's arm and told him that it was a shark, probably a basking shark, which I knew were native to the area. Øystein was just as excited by this news as he was when he thought it was a dolphin. We watched for a moment, until the fin slid from sight, and then we returned to our work. At first I thought that that would be the end of it.

"It was later that evening that it attacked us for the first time."

Dr Arnold hesitated as he prepared to take Dahlen's blood pressure. "The shark *attacked* the freighter?"

Dahlen nodded. "Yes. It must have been about eight o'clock in the evening when there was an almighty clanging noise from down below. It was like a church bell, only underwater. My first assumption was that we had struck a sea mine. We knew that…German…submarines were operating in the area, and that some of them were capable of laying sea mines. Myself, the captain - a grey-bearded man by the name of Otness - and some of the men went down into the hold to examine the damage.

"We were not taking in any water but the hull was…it was definitely damaged. The metal had been pushed in and then pinched together, jutting and stretched about six feet into the hold."

"Pushed in and pinched?" asked the doctor. "You mean the shark…?"

"Yes, doctor. The shark had attempted to bite the boat; and had managed to twist and bend steel in doing so. Of course, at the time, we did not even consider the possibility of the shark being responsible. Truth be told, I had almost forgotten ever seeing the beast."

"What did you think had caused the damage?" asked Krauser.

Dahlen shrugged. "We are…were…not military men, Captain Krauser. For all we knew, that was what sea mine damage looked like. After asserting that we would not be taking in any water - at least for a little while - we left it until the following morning to take a look at the exterior damage, and carry out any repairs as necessary.

"The following morning, two of the engineers went out in a life boat, and went underwater in scuba gear. You know scuba gear, yes? Good. They came up and reported that the metal was buckled, but there was no sign of heat damage, which ruled out the possibility of a sea mine, as far as we could tell. One of the men, Marcus, held up something he had found, though. It was a tooth."

"A shark's tooth?"

"It looked like the tooth of a shark, but…"

"But what, Mr Dahlen?"

Dahlen fished a sodden packet of cigarettes from his pocket and flung them aside with disgust. "Once I met a sailor who had the tooth of a Great White Shark polished and made into a pendant. He claimed that he had killed the shark himself, although I have no doubt that he actually picked up the thing in a tacky marketplace somewhere. Shore leave, most likely. It was large, Captain, probably seven or eight centimetres long."

"I have seen such teeth."

"The tooth Marcus held out that day was easily twice that size. It was…monstrous. Captain Otness paled when he saw it, and muttered that it could not be possible.

"The next day continued without any sign or sound of our shark, until finally, again at around eight at night, we saw it. Marcus – the man who discovered the tooth – and I were having a cigarette on deck, when we heard an almighty splash, and turned just in time to see the creature's fin break the water. Captain, this thing must be nearly thirty metres long. We saw it swim in a broad circle before submerging again.

"'Should we tell the Captain of this?' I asked.

"Marcus was rattled, but simply shrugged. 'What is there to tell him? And if we do, what can he do with the information? There are sometimes sharks in these waters, and this is just a large one.'

"I knew he was just attempting bravado, as we both knew this was no ordinary shark. About half an hour later, the thing attacked us again. Why it chose to follow us, and to attack us, I don't know. Maybe it could sense or smell the food in the cargo. Maybe we were just in its territory. This attack was much more aggressive than the first. It must have rammed us two or three times. I lost my footing with each strike, even when I managed to grab a hold of a rail or other fixing. Some of the men grabbed rifles and harpoons in the hope of killing the monster, but I do not think that such a thing can be done with weapons so small."

"When, at last, the attack subsided, some of us once again went below decks to examine the damage. It was much worse this time. We were taking in water; slowly, for sure, but enough to cause concern. The metal of the hull had been mangled, chewed…Captain, the power in that thing's jaws is simply unbelievable. Can you imagine trying to crumple the steel of a freighter with your teeth…your bare hands? I'd not hesitate to say that you would struggle to do it even with tools of your choice at your disposal."

"A G7a steam-driven torpedo seems to have made short of work of it."

Dahlen laughed. "After all I have told you so far do you *still* think that your torpedo is what sunk the *Freyr*, Captain? Maybe one of your torpedoes did hit us, but I can assure you that none of us noticed. We were all rather preoccupied, you see."

"What happened?" asked Dr Arnold, breathlessly. The doctor had stopped his examination of Dahlen, completely enraptured in his story for now.

"At about nine-thirty, nine-forty five this evening…" he checked his watch, only to find it was busted. "What time is it, please?"

Krauser checked his own wristwatch. "Eleven pm, or thereabouts."

"My god, has it only been an hour or so? How so much can change in so little time. Around then myself and Øystein were in the cargo hold, jerry rigging some repairs to stop the water coming in. It was secure, but still required some upkeep. The night was calm at first…but then it came."

-SIX-

Dr Arnold had finished his examination of their captive, having found no injuries beyond scrapes and bruises. He was concerned about the possibility of cold and shock, however, and had helped Dahlen out of his soaking wet clothes before wrapping him in a woollen blanket to stave off the chill of the North Sea. An ensign arrived with a mug of warm coffee which he handed to him. Dahlen nodded his thanks and sipped the exceedingly bitter liquid with a grimace.

"The coffee is awful. My apologies," smiled Dr Arnold.

Dahlen nodded, before continuing his story. "We had no warning. Well, looking back now, I think I could hear something. Almost as though I could hear water rushing, or the pressure building up, on the other side of the hull. I thought nothing of it at the time, and even if I had, I don't believe that there is anything I could have done to help the *Freyr* escape its fate. Øystein was right by the weak spot, examining some of the damaged rivets in one of the braces. I remember there was a trickle of water running from one or two of them, and although the flow was very gentle, it was already causing the paint to bubble and warp. Then, seemingly from nowhere, there was an explosion."

Krauser nodded. "As I said: the torpedo."

Dahlen shook his head. "Forget your torpedo, Captain. I am sorry to rob you of your victory and pride, but what I saw was not man made.

"The wall of the hold just...burst open. The metal split and pushed inwards, as though some giant had fixed it with a bayonet. The walls peeled upwards and split as the shark forced its way in. Captain...the size of this thing. It looked like the devil himself had taken shark form. It was faded grey...maybe even white in places. One dead black eye stared into the room; it must have lost the other in some battles months, perhaps even decades past, as all that remained was a sod of lumpy scar tissue. The head of the shark pushed its way into the hold and we felt the entire ship shift under its weight, causing the floor to become a slope directly into the things mouth.

"I was fortunate enough to grab a hold of a support pillar. The steel held, despite the chaos."

Dahlen sat for a moment, lost in his memory. Eventually Krauser grew uncomfortable in the silence and felt the need to push him along. "And Øystein?"

Dahlen breathed in deeply, and blew it out shakily. "Øystein was...not so fortunate. He lost his footing as the sea water cascaded in. The floor turned into a slide under the salt water and the deadly angle the shark created. He went straight onto his backside, and...slid straight to the beast. The shark opened its jaw and...Captain, its mouth must have opened three metres wide. Not that that was the worst part.

"Sharks have more than one set of teeth you know. They have rows and rows of them, like a meat grinder. Almost as soon as one is lost, the next can roll forward to fill the gap. This jaw spread open three metres, let out a gust of disgusting, rotting breath, and those teeth…

"Øystein slid in feet first. He managed to catch hold of the thing's bottom lip, and tried to kick and lever himself out, but it did no good. Those jaws came together with a suctioning *boom*, and Øystein screamed as the teeth drove into his thighs, broke his legs, ripped at his stomach. He slid in another half a metre, and they came down again, crushing his rib cage this time. He vomited a gout of blood which only seemed to ignite the beast's hunger further. Two more chomps in rapid succession and Øystein was dead. Two more and he was gone from sight. The thing ate him whole, Captain."

Dr Arnold looked terrified. "My god, if what you say is true, this thing is…simply colossal. Captain, can a shark really puncture through the steel of a tanker? Can they grow to that size?"

Krauser paused and took a deep breath before continuing. "I am not an expert on sharks, doctor, but I do not believe that Mr Dahlen is lying. I am sorry for the loss of your friend, Øystein, Mr Dahlen."

Dahlen waved his hand in part acknowledgement, part dismissal. "He was not exactly a friend, but he was a young man, and I was sorry to see him go. Especially in so grotesque a manner."

"Please continue your story."

"The shark retreated once it had consumed Øystein, and slid back into the dark waters. Immediately the cold sea poured in through the hole it had torn, and I was left drenched and freezing. Instantly I felt the boat lurch hard to the side, and I knew that we had to be sinking. I ran for the ladder back to the upper decks. I slowly made my way there by bouncing off and grabbing onto struts and packing crates and chains, the water making my every step laborious. When I at last reached the ladder, the hold shuddered as if in a seizure, and once again the shark came for me. It caught and scratched its skin on the shredded metal of the opening, but this did not seem to bother it in the slightest. I felt myself tremble under the gaze of that dead eye once more, before the adrenaline kicked in and I was up the ladder and on deck before I knew what was happening.

"Captain Otness was leading the evacuation. Like yourself, he assumed that it was a torpedo that had hit us. I tried to tell him what had happened, but he could not hear me in the chaos of the men readying the lifeboats for escape. He waved me off and shoved me in the direction of the nearest lifeboat, and I followed this order.

"Once we were in the boat, it seemed to crash down through the darkness and onto the water. Two of the men – I forget their names already – rowed us as far away from the ship as we could get. They feared a fire reaching the fuel reserves, or something of that nature, I suppose. I didn't tell them what the real thing to fear was. Who of them would have believed me?"

Dahlen fell silent for a moment, and sipped his coffee. When he continued, the panic that had been edging into his voice had subsided, and he was back to his normal, almost stoic, manner. "I did not see the first lifeboat go down. I don't know that anyone did. I heard some of the men shout that the boat was missing. At first they called for their friends, hoping that they were just adrift in the darkness. Perhaps some of them feared they had capsized, or something, but in my heart, I already knew what had happened…and I knew it was only a matter of time until our boat was next."

"We saw what happened to the other lifeboats," said Krauser. "We were making our way toward you to provide assistance when your boat was sunk. We feared you were lost to the shark, until we spotted you clinging to that driftwood."

"I have no idea how I survived, myself," replied Dahlen. "I do not even really remember the shark hitting our lifeboat. Well, I do, but it is…sort of in a dream. Or rather a nightmare, eh? I remember our boat being…thrown up, I suppose…though it actually felt more as though the boat was *pushed* upwards. I did not see the shark. I just saw the foam and spray, heard the shouts of my colleagues…but I smelled that same death and rotten fish odour that I remembered from the cargo hold. Then I crashed into the water, and…to be honest, the next thing I really remember is being helped aboard your ship."

"Boat."

"Sorry?"

"We are a boat, not a ship. A minor technicality, but a bugbear of most submarine crews."

Dahlen nodded in understanding. Dr Arnold turned to Krauser to offer his diagnosis. "He's in shock, and there's possibly a slight concussion, but nothing serious. Keep him warm and dry and rested for a day or two and he'll be in perfect health."

Krauser nodded. "Mr Dahlen, we will hand you over to the Kriegsmarine when we return home at the end of this patrol in a week or so. They will arrange your safe return back to your family."

"Thank you, Captain. I appreciate your hospitality. And I hope that we make it 'home'."

Krauser left the man with the doctor, and made his way back to the control room. He knew what Dahlen was inferring. If this shark had indeed sunk a freighter, then what chance did the U-616 stand?

-SEVEN-

August Krauser finally hit his bunk several hours later; it must have been about three o clock in the morning when he finally turned in. His sleep was dark and dreamless, and yet he still felt fatigued upon waking, and it took two mugs of the submarine's glutinous coffee before he was truly feeling ready for duty. At about eleven o'clock in the morning, he was reading in his bunk when Hertz approached him with news that a new target had been sighted.

He was surprised. It could be days between spotting viable targets; and even then it was not always feasible to launch an attack. The ship could be escorted, or travelling too fast, weather could be against them, or the target could simply be too small to be worth expending the ammunition.

Krauser headed on deck with his second in command, suppressing a shiver, having once again left his windbreaker by his bunk. He peered through his binoculars, and could see that the freighter on the horizon would indeed make a viable target. It was certainly large – perhaps slightly larger than the *Freyr* had been the day before, and he gave the command to Hertz to close to torpedo range. "Dive immediately at the first sign of an escort."

"Yes, sir."

They retired to the hot and noisy control room as the U-616 sped through the waters, in pursuit of its quarry. Hertz gave him a smile. "We are lucky to have two hunts in twenty-four hours. This will keep the men better motivated than any chess tournament."

Krauser nodded. He didn't like it, but he knew he was right. The men needed to blow off steam on a patrol, and if the steam came packaged in a G7a torpedo, then so be it. After half an hour or so the submarine slowed down, and seemed to come to a near stop. They had reached torpedo range.

Krauser looked through the periscope at the target ship. It was actually a tanker, rather than a freighter – Admiral Dönitz would be pleased if they managed to bag this particular trophy. Depriving the British of fuel for their planes and vehicles would aid Germany greatly. "Any sign of an escort?" he asked.

"No, captain. She's alone," replied one of the men.

Krauser nodded. "She's far too large a target to risk the deck gun. Load four steam torpedoes into the forward tubes."

The command was shouted along the length of the submarine. The men working the torpedo tubes hurriedly swung their payload along, the room filling with clamour and organised chaos. In less than a minute the four tubes were locked and loaded, ready to deliver death and destruction to their target.

After giving the men two minutes to organise themselves, Krauser called "Fire one!"

The ship shuddered as the torpedo spat forth, pushed through the water by compressed steam. Krauser could see the bubble jets as it sped towards the tanker. He waited, and counted under his breath, knowing that everyone in the control room was doing the same thing. As he hit fifty, he saw a huge gout of water and flame shoot from the side of the tanker. A rewarding, percussive sound followed half a second later. "Direct hit!" he yelled, and the men in the control room cheered in victory. "Fire two and three!"

The submarine shuddered once more, more intensely this time, as two torpedoes were fired in rapid succession. Again the Captain of the U-616 watched the jets bubble across the ocean, counting under his breath. Another blossoming of water and flame told him that at least one of the torpedoes had successfully reached its mark, and that another target was succumbing to the might of the finest war machine in the Kriegsmarine.

"Direct hit!" he cried again. Cheers of celebration, "Kriegsmarine!" and "Heil Hitler!" filled the room once more. "Come, Mr Hertz. Let's head up top!"

He hurried up the ladder to the main deck, followed by the older second-in-command. He suppressed a shiver and watched through his binoculars at the burning ship. "Another victory for the U-616!" he said to Hertz.

Hertz smiled. "Yes, sir. To the glory of the Fuhrer, and the Fatherland!"

Krauser did not. He was not so stupid as to speak openly against the Nationalsozialistische Deutsche Arbeiterpartei and his nation's leader, but he did not particularly care for their politics himself, and neither did the majority of his crew. His job was the same regardless of who held the Reichstag, or how they managed to get in there in the first place. Hertz was obviously a devotee of Adolf Hitler, but that was his own business.

The other reason he didn't reply was that something seemed off to him. There was a tension or pressure in the air, that hadn't been there before. Something had caused the hairs on his arms and the back of his neck to rise. He scanned the water, nervously, involuntarily. Dahlen's tale of his battle with the shark must have gotten under his skin, that's all…

Except it wasn't all. He could definitely hear something now; something that was not normally there. A high pitched, buzzing that seemed to be coming from somewhere…up above?

He span just in time to see the Sunderland screaming out of the cloud cover, its machine guns sending up a spray of searing hot lead as it began a strafing run of the U-Boat. Milliseconds later the bullets rained all around him. Time seemed to slow down into a series of very short motion pictures. Two of the crew ran for the deck gun, but were cut down, blood gouting from their arms and chests as the bullets struck. Wood splinters flew as stray rounds thudded into the deck. Hertz slid down the ladder, rapidly disappearing from view. There was a beastly roar as the plane shot over head. He knew he had only seconds before it turned for a second pass.

Three, no, four men now lay dead on the deck. No time to check identities, he would have to take a roll call when – if – they managed to escape the Sunderland. He screamed "Alarm!" as he slid down the ladder into the comparative warmth and darkness of the control room. Bells rang and whistles shrieked in the wave of this command.

The U-616 began its crash dive.

The men worked in unison, as much a well-oiled machine as the U-Boat itself. Cogs span, dive planes were adjusted, and the tanks began to fill with sea water, causing the ship to rapidly sink beneath the surface. In less than a minute, they were submerged, and still diving. The Type VIIB U-Boat was pressure tested to a depth of two hundred and twenty metres, and it was a brave captain indeed who would exceed this measurement in all but a life or death situation.

The crew fell silent, as was standard practice, fearing that the slightest noise could be detected by enemy ships operating in the areas. As one, Krasuer, Kleiner, Hertz, the entire crew (including Dr Arnold and Dahlen in the rear of the boat) turned their gaze upwards. Krauser never knew why this was. The deadliest depth charges always came from the side or – worse – from below, yet every seaman he knew (himself included) involuntarily looked up when threatened by them. A depth charge was a submarine's deadliest enemy.

"One hundred and fifty metres deep," whispered Kleiner.

"Hold steady," Krauser replied.

Two hollow splashes told them that the Sunderland had dropped depth charges, and there was nothing that the crew of the U-616 could do now, but wait.

The seconds dragged like hours as everyone aboard fell silent, before the first shock hit. It came from the starboard side, and the entire boat tilted on its axis, and skidded sideways. Men shouted, metal screamed, and Krauser gritted his teeth so hard he feared they might shatter in his mouth. In a deadly one-two punch, the U-616 was thrown sideways and careered into the second depth charge. This one hit so hard on the underside that Dahlen grabbed hold of the doctor and shouted that the shark had come back for them. Krauser felt himself thrown upwards by the sheer force of the depth charge, lost his footing and seemed to float momentarily before landing hard on his right arm. He screamed as a terrible, muscular pain flared white hot just above the elbow. He feared that it had been broken.

Kleiner mistook his scream for a shout of "Dive!" and the order was hurriedly relayed as the captain staggered back to his feet. The first he knew of the mistake was when he cleared his head and Kleiner reported that U-616 was now holding steady at two hundred metres.

Another splash heralded the dropping of another depth charge, but either U-616 had moved sufficiently far away, or the Sunderland had miscalculated their position. Krauser gave the order to travel submerged for a good couple of hours before sending the periscope up to check the coast was clear.

"Yes, sir," replied Kleiner, adding, "Captain, you are bleeding."

Krauser looked down, and saw that the right sleeve of his shirt was completely saturated with blood.

-EIGHT-

The damage to the U-616 was extensive, even without taking into account the four men dead from the Sunderland's original strafing run. Krauser sat on his bunk as Dr Arnold tended to his arm. It turned out that it was not broken, but that he had in fact taken a bullet from the Sunderland. He had obviously been so distracted by the action around him ("adrenaline", the doctor called it) that he hadn't noticed at the time. Dr Arnold was able to remove the bullet, but the wound still hurt like crazy.

After a couple of hours running silently beneath the waves, Krauser gave the order to surface and begin repairs. He left Hertz in charge of the control room, and lay on his bunk with a bottle of whiskey, to try and rest and blot out the pain of his new gunshot wound.

He couldn't deny that he felt a palpable sense of relief upon surfacing. He was never fazed by being underwater – one could hardly rise to the position of captain aboard a U-Boat if one was – but after a tense experience like being depth charged, it felt like literally coming up for air.

He managed to doze a little over the course of two hours while the men carried out their preliminary repairs. This time his dreams were dark and fitful, full of sudden explosions and dark teeth in the water. He was in particular haunted by the dead black eyes of the Great White Shark he had seen on shore leave, and the spinning driftwood of the *Freyr*'s lifeboats.

He was eventually brought fully awake by Kleiner at his bedside. "Sir?"

Krauser blinked away sleep and pushed himself up using his injured arm, causing him to groan between gritted teeth. "Yes, what is it?"

"I have the damage report, sir."

The captain rubbed his eyes and nodded. "Tell me."

"We've lost ten men in all, sir. The four men up on the deck, two were crushed when a torpedo broke loose in the launching bay and four more suffered head or neck injuries as a result of being thrown about in the explosion, sir."

Krauser groaned. Of a crew of forty-two, that was a substantial loss. "Get names for me. I will write the letters to their families. And prepare them for burial."

A ship as tightly packed as a Type VII U-Boat didn't have the capacity for a morgue, and all the men knew that. In the event of their death, they would be buried at sea. The phrase "fish food" leapt into Krauser's mind, followed by the glimpses he had had of the shark that had demolished the crew of the *Freyr* (and the *Freyr* itself, if Dahlen could be believed).

Kleiner nodded before continuing with his report. "Yes, sir. Also, the flak gun is inoperable, and two of the forward torpedo tubes are jammed. We still have two in front, two in rear and the deck gun, sir. They, at least, are all fully operational. Unfortunately, the manoeuvring planes are damaged. We can rise and dive okay, but our speed and manoeuvrability are not what they should be. In short, if we run into trouble again…I don't know that we'll be able to get out of it so easily. We'd struggle to get away from a destroyer, and another Sunderland would have us dead in the water, sir. Hell, if we run into that shark again I-"

"What?"

"Nothing, sir. I was just making a little joke."

"Are the crew concerned about the shark? Genuinely, I mean."

Kleiner hesitated before replying. "I've heard some of the men talking about it, sir. There seems to be a feeling that if it could destroy a freighter, then it would make short work of the U-616."

"The North Sea is a very large body of water, Mr Kleiner. Our chances of encountering the same shark again are minimal; and I have to say that I don't like my crew being frightened of sea monsters. I want you to quash these sentiments wherever they arise. Do I make myself clear?"

"Yes, Captain, sir."

"What else?"

"There is one last thing, sir."

Krauser grabbed his cigarettes and matches, feeling the need for a smoke on deck. "Oh? And what is that?"

"There is a fracture in the hull. We took in a little water. Nothing major, and we managed to pump it out and patch it up. We're stable again, but…I really don't think we should push our luck in the event of another attack."

"You mean the water pressure?"

"Yes, sir. I wouldn't like to hazard a guess as to how far we could dive safely, but…just not too far, if you follow me, sir."

"I do. Thank you, Mr Kleiner."

After dismissing the chief engineer, Krauser headed to see Dahlen, the Norwegian "prisoner of war". "How are you doing, Mr Dahlen?"

The Norwegian man was now occupying one of the dead men's bunks, reading a battered and foxed novel he had found, attempting to drink another viscous coffee. For a man used to working in the wind and spray, he had adapted remarkably well to the noise, stink and humidity of the submarine. To see him relaxing with a coffee and a book, he looked like a gentleman on holiday, rather than a prisoner and recent torpedo and then shark attack survivor. He looked up, his eyes flitting momentarily to Krauser's bandaged arm. "I am better than you, it would appear. Did you cut yourself shaving?"

Krauser laughed. The deadpan humour was somehow even funnier in Dahlen's Norwegian accent. It was hard not to like the man. "A little gift from a fleeting visitor."

Dahlen nodded. "When the explosions started, I thought they had us. Is it always that terrifying?"

Krauser was stone faced. "Yes. Always. You know, I think that this must be worse than being shot at in a combat zone, or in a dogfight with a Spitfire. There you can dodge. You can return fire. You can call on your comrades for assistance. You can at least see or sense where the enemy *is*. A U-Boat is different. We attack out of darkness, and when we are attacked, we sit in darkness, waiting to see if it is our turn to die."

"So, what was it that made you want to work in a submarine?"

"I'm not sure. A series of choices and events that led me to a job that I do not particularly enjoy, but that I do not hate, either. It is as such with most men, yes?"

"Indeed. How bad was the damage?"

"It is not good. I am considering returning for home. We simply don't have the equipment available to repair it here, and both our offensive and defensive capabilities are hampered."

"Then we are heading home early?"

"I said I was considering it."

Dahlen nodded, thinking for a moment. "What will you do if we run into the shark again?"

Krauser hardened his gaze. "I do not think that will be an issue. I am truly sorry for the fate that befell the *Freyr*, but the North Sea is a large body of water, Mr Dahlen, and we are a relatively small boat. I think it exceedingly unlikely that our paths will cross again."

"Captain Krauser, do you forget my story so quickly? The beast followed our freighter for three days, travelling at a speed that I would imagine far exceeds any that your vessel is capable of. If it has decided to hunt us, then it will catch us. You can count on that. Do you intend to torpedo the thing before it crushes your hull in its jaws?"

"The shark is not hunting us. The Kriegsmarine is the hunter of these waters."

"The Hunter can become The Hunted."

"Mr Dahlen, supposing that the shark could track us, why on Earth should it want to? The *Freyr* left a large wake, and was carrying fresh produce, which the thing could eat. We are a war machine. We leave no wake. We have done nothing to pique its interest and we have done nothing to provoke it. Frankly, Mr Dahlen, I see no reason why your shark should have noticed the U-616 at all. Please, put it from your mind. Regardless of my decision, we will be home within a week, and your shark will be far behind us."

Dahlen nodded. "I hope you are right, captain. Because – believe me – if this shark wants the U-616, it *will* take it."

***

The repairs were carried out as quickly and as fully as was feasible, but the majority of the damage – the serious damage - simply could not be repaired either with the tools they had at their disposal, or without taking the ship into a dry dock.

Krauser conducted the funeral service on deck for the ten members of the crew that had not survived the depth charge attack. He did it almost by rote, straight from the manual. Truth be told, most of the men had been new to the crew for this patrol, and he was not close to any of them. In war, it took a while before you bothered to get close to people. It simply wasn't worth the effort if they were not going to survive. It was cold and it was cruel, but it was the way that things were.

The submarine steamed through the ocean, and the bodies were thrown off of the side, one by one.

Leaving a trail of fresh meat in its wake.

-NINE-

The submarine was coasting slowly through the waters as the sun touched the horizon, the sky streaking into purple and orange. Dahlen and Krauser were smoking and conversing by the deck gun as ten or so of the crew milled around, some repairing some of the minor damage from the depth charge attack, the others relaxing, or cleaning the decks. Their hammering, clanging and chatting was a gentle white noise, mixed with the constant hiss of the waves against the hull of the ship. The wind was a nice breeze, and it was not too cold for a change. Krauser was grateful for this, having once again left his windbreaker by his bunk.

"Will the men not think it odd you are fraternising with the enemy?" asked Dahlen.

Krauser chuckled. "If anyone asks, I'm escorting a prisoner."

Dahlen accepted a cigarette from the captain, and lit it. "Do you have anyone waiting for you at home?"

"My wife. We have a child on the way. It should be born when I'm next on home leave."

"That is good timing."

"It was more accident than design, but as you say, good timing, either way. Yourself?"

"My wife, two sons."

They were prevented from talking for the moment by a vigorous hammering noise as Herkenhoff - one of the youngest recruits - took a heavy lump hammer to a handrail that had been bent out of shape. They watched the rhythmic pounding for a while, noticing long before the ensign did that the rail was refusing to budge. "Herkenhoff!"

The young ensign turned, and Krauser suppressed a smile as he saw the young man's shock at being addressed directly by his captain. "Yes, Captain?"

"Try it from the other side."

"Yes, Captain!"

Herkenhoff went to climb over the guard rail to attack it from the water side, causing Dahlen to wince and Krauser to yell out once again, "Herkenhoff!"

The eighteen year old turned again, eyes wide, one leg over the rail as if he were hopping over a style on a countryside walk. "Yes, Captain?"

"Get a damn rope and secure yourself first. I've lost enough men to the sea for one day, thank you."

"Yes…yes, Captain," he replied, heading off to find some rope.

"Youth thinks it is immortal," muttered Dahlen.

Krauser chuckled. "You see the job I have here? Warrior, leader, office manager and –

occasionally – school master. Did you see his eyes?"

"He looked as though he was worried you were going to cane him, or give him a detention."

Krauser laughed out loud. "Exactly! Fresh out of school, and out on the ocean. Poor man. Boy. Whatever."

Dahlen exhaled a cloud of smoke. "Here he comes again."

Herkenhoff carried a length of rope, one end of which he fastened around a hard point on the opposite side of the deck from where he intended to hop the rail. Aware that he was under the watchful eye of his captain, it was obvious that he was being doubly sure in everything he did. Truth be told, he checked the rope was fast two or three times more than he needed to, but at least Krauser had no grounds on which he could properly berate the boy. He carried the rope across the deck to the battered handrail, and tied a loop around his body, from his left shoulder to his right hip, like a royal sash.

His confidence buoyed by the fact that neither his captain nor any of his other superiors up on deck that evening had said anything, he grabbed the rail in both hands, and confidently climbed over it. His ankles were at near-on a forty-five angle against the hull of the ship, but he was able to hold the rail in his right hand, and his hammer in the left, leaving him confident enough he would not slip into the water – and if he did, at least there was the added security of the rope.

"Much better, Mr Herkenhoff!"

"Yes, Captain."

The two men watched the boy at work for a moment, before Dahlen asked "Have you given any more thought as to what you will do next?"

Krauser sighed. "I don't like it, but we may have to turn back. I expect you to keep this to yourself, but the radio was also damaged in the attack. If we end up in a worse situation, or in dire need of support, we have no means of calling for help. I dare say that I'll receive a dressing down from my superiors for being overly cautious, but I won't risk the lives of my crew any more than I absolutely need to."

"You're a good man, Captain Krauser. This is the right d-"

A deafening explosion of water fountaining up from the starboard side of the deck interrupted whatever Dahlen had been going to say. The Norwegian fell backwards, instinctively covering his head with his hands. "What the…?"

Krauser was forced to grab hold of the deck gun for support, but managed to hold his footing. The colossal fountain of water made him think that the submarine had been torpedoed, or that they had struck a sea mine – just his luck when they were already so critically damaged!

He heard the thudding and rattling of men running around the wooden deck, and the screaming of at least one injured man. He smelt salt water and – no, not cordite or burning - he smelt rotting fish and the iron tang of blood. His arm hairs rose and he knew what he was going to see before his eyes gained focus upon it.

A cold, genetic memory of fear ran through him as he saw the leviathan up close for the first time.

Its flesh was blubber and muscle, an old, washed out grey, similar to a Great White, five times larger. Its mouth was a funnel of blood and sharp knives. The largest teeth themselves were twenty-five centimetres long, some brown and broken, some white; all sharp as glass and as hard as diamond. The monster's one, black eye stared sightlessly along the deck, giving the impression that it was not vision that guided its vicious attacks, but rather some otherworldly sense of prescience.

Its skin was a mass of scar tissue, telling tales of the battles it had fought and won years, decades, perhaps centuries in the past. It had seen much and defeated enemies and history alike. Krauser could not shake the impression that this was some throwback to prehistory. A relic of a shark, some monster from before humanity or even the dinosaurs had walked the earth, before life itself had crawled out of the ocean.

This white ghost of oceans past's name was Death, and it had come for the U-616.

The shark was rising up the side of the hull, and it was just as big as Dahlen had claimed. Only its head up to its - for want of a better term - neck was visible, but the jaws had to be three metres wide. Young Herkenhoff was trapped in them from the legs down, screaming blue murder and struggling against his grisly fate. Each attempt he made to wriggle from the thing's maw only caused a hundred teeth the size of meat cleavers to dig in and brutalise him further.

The shark let out a soundless grunt and Krauser retched as the stench hit him. He snatched his Mauser from his belt and took a few pot shots at the shark, desperately attempting to force it to let Herkenhoff go. Small puffs and gouts of red mist showed where his rounds had struck, but the shark gave little sign that it had noticed. Its jaws merely mashed up and down a few times, causing Herkenhoff's screams to shoot up an octave.

Dahlen grabbed him by the arm and shouted "That pea shooter won't do a thing! Do you have a harpoon? A bill hook? Anything up here?"

No. Of course they didn't. They were a war machine, not a fishing vessel. Krauser shoved the man aside and – bravado and adrenaline overruling his common sense, charged directly at the shark, pulling a large knife from his belt.

The shark let out another gust of foul air, Herkenhoff screamed again, and then the shark slid back into the cold dark water, dragging the poor ensign with it. As it swam away with its meal, the rope still attached to Herkenhoff pulled taut and swung fast across the deck like a clothesline. Dahlen caught it full force in the chest, and was knocked to the deck, winded. Three of the crew were ensnared around their legs and ankles and were sent into the sea with a scream.

With a quick ripping and snapping sound the rope broke free, and shot off into the ocean. Krauser ran to the entrance to the command room and screamed that there was a man overboard. Instantly, three, four, five men came dashing up the ladder to assist. Of the three men that were thrown into the water, only one was pulled out. Of the other two, there was no sign, but Krauser knew in his heart that the shark had taken them. A three course meal, courtesy of the U-616.

***

As the sun sank halfway below the horizon, Dahlen and Krauser once again smoked by the deck gun, although this time, they were sat on the wooden deck, leaning their backs against the gun itself. After half an hour or more of silence, Dahlen said "Let me guess...it was bigger than you expected?"

-TEN-

"Captain, we have to abandon this patrol. Nearly half the crew are dead. Vital operational systems are damaged, along with the radio itself. We must return home. To remain out here is suicide."

Hertz wasn't telling Krauser anything that he didn't already know. He was embarrassed that one of his patrols should have to terminate early, but he consoled himself that it was more or less entirely due to circumstances beyond his control. Taking on survivors, a strafing run, a depth charge and being attacked by a colossal shark all in one day were not covered in the officer's training manual.

"I am aware of the situation we are in, Mr Hertz. However, you must consider my position. It is not you who will receive the sharp end of it should we return early. I have a lot of things to weigh up before making such a decision. Now, I say to you again: I have faith in my men, and I have faith in my equipment. All I ask is that they have faith in me in return."

Hertz's eye twitched, and it was obvious that he did not have the faith in him that he did a mere twenty-four hours ago.

"Is there a problem, Mr Hertz?"

"No, sir," the older man replied, tightly. "There is no problem."

"Please take the control room. I have work of my own to see to."

"Sir."

Hertz turned on his heel and made his way down the crowded corridor as quickly as he was able – which was to say 'not very'. A submarine is always in motion, with people coming and going and squeezing through tiny doors and small gaps. Krauser watched him go, with a sigh. A calm, Norwegian voice spoke from the space by his head. "He does not like you."

Krauser turned to see Dahlen, still reading his grotty novel in his bunk. He didn't bother to look up to see Krauser's reaction. The captain let out a sigh and said, "No. No, he doesn't."

"What is his problem this time?"

"He thinks we should return home, and – as I said to you upstairs - he has a point. I know in my heart he is right, but my pride doesn't like it. The boat is badly damaged, including weapons, manoeuvrability and our radio. If we run into a target, we can't engage it. If we run into a plane or destroyer, it will sink us."

"And there is a shark trying to eat us."

"Oh, come, man! A freak attack doesn't mean that that thing is still loitering out there waiting to-"

Dahlen looked up from his book and said nothing.

"Yes. All right. A shark is trying to eat us."

"You believe my story, now?"

"I never disbelieved your story in general, Dahlen, but…yes. Now I have seen the beast I believe all of it. This thing is clever. It's agile. It's powerful. It…"

"It is large."

"Large? I've never conceived of a shark so large. What is it?"

Dahlen shrugged. "It is hungry. Is that not all that is important?"

Krauser sighed. "Smoke on deck with me?"

"Of course."

***

The breeze felt good after the cloying humidity of the interior of the U-616. The sun was just rising, making the sea turn blood red as Dahlen and Krauser stood against the rail, watching the ocean for any signs of their quarry – or any signs of what hunted them.

"Have you decided what you are to do? What will win out? Your heart or your head?" asked Dahlen, flicking his cigarette end into the ocean, and lighting another.

"I am still undecided," sighed Krauser. "Although I suppose I know that turning back is the only option. We cannot continue like this. I will not – I cannot - risk my men's lives any more than I have already."

Dahlen nodded, his gaze on the horizon. "There is an alternative."

"And what is that?"

"We go fishing."

Krauser chuckled, but stopped when he saw the granite face of the prisoner. "You are serious?"

"You have firepower and armour here. I say we hunt that which hunts us."

"You mean…?"

"Yes. I say we stay here and kill this thing."

Krauser laughed - a full laugh, this time. "My friend, Admiral Dönitz is not paying us to explode sharks."

"He is not paying you to bring home unspent torpedoes, either. How many torpedoes does this ship carry?"

"We start our patrol with a full complement of fourteen torpedoes; a mixture of steam and electric driven."

Dahlen turned, and leant his back against the railing, inhaling on his cigarette. "And that thing?" he asked, indicating the deck gun.

"Two hundred and twenty rounds. Eighty-eight millimetre. It only works against surface targets, though."

Dahlen shrugged. "We've both seen this thing surface. Now, how many torpedoes would you say that you expend in a single attack on a vessel? The *Freyr*, for example."

"We fired three torpedoes on the *Freyr*, although I was ready to fire more. The torpedoes have their strengths, you see. When a torpedo hits, it hits very hard indeed. They have good range. We can fire them unseen by the target. Between you and I, however, they are far from reliable. I don't know what the official figures are, but in my experience around half of the rounds we carry are duds, or they fail to make the range of their target, or something drifts them off course. They have their strengths, Mr Dahlen, but they have many weaknesses, also."

Dahlen considered this for a moment. "Fourteen torpedoes...say four a target...so you could only really sink three or four ships a patrol?"

Krauser had never really considered it like that. "Yes, I suppose so. Sometimes we are able to use the Deck Gun, or sometimes we bag more on a good patrol, but yes, three or four would be satisfactory to me."

"So, it wouldn't be unusual for you to return home with all of your torpedoes spent?"

"Uncommon, but not unusual. It certainly wouldn't raise eyebrows, if that's what you're thinking."

"And the deck gun?"

"They'd be surprised if we'd burned through over two hundred rounds of the thing, but it wouldn't be uncommon to have fired off more than a few."

"And the radio is out, you say?"

Krauser flicked his cigarette butt into the sea, momentarily getting a vision of a toothed maw leaping from it to claim him, and suppressed a shiver. "Yes. No contact in or out."

"Then why don't we go fishing? We can spend a few days here…we could drop anchor, or whatever the submarine equivalent is. Whether or not we kill this thing, your commanders will think nothing of you burning through some rounds of ammunition. Time it right, and you'll be back home when you should be. Who would be to know that you didn't complete your patrol as planned? The men are hardly going to report that you ordered they spend several days in pursuit of a sea monster, are they?"

Krauser had to admit that Dahlen made a very strong argument. It was hardly within his mission parameters to eliminate marine life, no matter how much of a grievance he or the Norwegian may have against it. Hertz would be a problem, too. He may go along with it at the time, but as soon as they got back to dry land he knew Hertz would be filling in all kinds of reports and pushing for a court martial, just to be a pain in the backside and further his own career. He needed work – his wife and unborn child depended on that. Could he really stop and take a break just to hunt sea monsters?

"I'm sorry, Mr Dahlen, but we cannot do that. People at home are depending on these men making it back home alive, and these men are depending on me to get them there. The U-616 is critically damaged, and we need to go home."

The usually laid back Norwegian man stiffened and his eyes widened a little. "Captain, this shark *is* hunting us. You know that. If we do not kill it, it will destroy the U-616 just as it destroyed the *Freyr* and God alone knows how many vessels before that. We are here, and we have the weapons to destroy it. You can save the lives of your men, and countless hundreds of others. Do you not see that this thing, this shark, this monster will continue to strike again and again?"

Krauser straightened and fixed Dahlen with a steely gaze. "Mr Dahlen. I like you. I like you, and I'm sorry for what happened to your ship, but the fact remains that you *are* a prisoner of war and you *are* aboard my boat, and *I* am the Captain. I have listened to your suggestions, and I have considered them…but we *are* going home. We are badly damaged, and if we do 'hunt' this shark…then people are going to die."

"And people will die if we do not!"

"*That* is not my concern, Mr Dahlen! The men below are my only concern right now and I say we're heading home."

Dahlen stopped and composed himself. "I'm sorry, Captain. You're right. We will do as you command."

***

Krauser headed to the command room and issued his orders to Hertz, who was barely able to suppress a smile at getting his own way for once. Unable to be around the man's smugness, and not especially wanting to be in Dahlen's company after their tiff on deck, he headed to his bunk, and dozed fitfully for a few hours. Once again, he dreamed dark, terrifying dreams. Dreams of the white ghost of ocean's past that followed them through the water, unseen.

-ELEVEN-

The next day, Krauser was working the command room with Kleiner and three of the men – numbers were naturally stretched thin, following the casualties that they had suffered – when they sighted the convoy. Convoys were a double edged sword for U-Boat crews. They were a target rich environment, full of large freighters and tankers, but they were almost always escorted by destroyers armed with deck guns and depth charges, capable of sending even the bravest submarine crew to the bottom of the ocean. Krauser was constantly aware that the submarine was in far from the best condition, and that a single run in with a destroyer could crush them with ease.

"As tempting as the targets may be, we cannot risk contact with the escort. Dive to periscope depth, and run silent. We shall wait until they have moved from visual range and then commence our journey home."

The men nodded and ran off to carry out his orders. Shouts and klaxons and bells rattled up and down the length of the boat as the U-616 submerged. After a while, the submarine finally fell silent, and Krauser felt the humidity and closeness all around him. He felt sweat crawl down his back, itching and tickling. He whispered to Kleiner "I say we give them twenty minutes, and then see what we can see."

Kleiner nodded, and stood silently, leaning back against the interior hull of the submarine, and closed his eyes. Even the purring of the electric engines faded and stopped. They were in silent running. The men were all quiet, either laying down, or standing still to conserve oxygen. So it remained for the next twenty minutes.

Krauser tried to keep his attention focused on the convoy, but twenty minutes was a long time to remain focused on one thing, and his mind naturally wandered. His thoughts turned to his arguments with Hertz, to his wife and family at home, to what would happen to Arild Dahlen when they finally reached home port. When he next checked his watch, he saw that it had actually been nearer to half an hour since they had submerged. He stepped up to the periscope, and span it up around the surface of the water, searching for the convoy. "There's no sign of the convoy…but…there's another ship."

"Close, Captain?" asked Kleiner.

"Six hundred metres, maybe. Small Freighter. No sign of an escort."

Kleiner hesitated before asking, "Should I prepare an attack, sir?"

Krauser knew that the ship would be easy pickings. It was a small vessel, only two thousand tonnes, if that. A direct hit from a torpedo – or perhaps even the deck gun - would smash it to pieces…but was that something that they could chance? "Negative, Mr Kleiner. We're still too close to that convoy. If this ship is able to radio through to their escort, we'll be dead in the wat-"

He hesitated as a faint rumble ran through the ship on the starboard side. Had one of the engines kicked back into life? No. There was no sound, or motion. Had they run aground? Against a rock, or something? Surely not.

"Did you feel that?" whispered one of the men in the reddened darkness of the silent control room. "Felt like a torpedo shot past us…"

Krauser felt a chill run through him.

"Could there be a Wolf Pack in the area we don't know about? Perhaps they've engaged this freighter?" asked another.

Wolf Packs were teams of three or more U-Boats that operated in unison, rather than the lone patrols carried out by the U-616. They were able to co-ordinate their attacks to knock out larger or grouped targets, and their numbers made it harder for destroyers or aircraft to locate them for a counter attack. With the U-616's radio being destroyed, they'd have no way of knowing if one was in the area or not.

"Captain, could there be a Wolf Pack?"

"That was no torpedo," replied Krauser in a hollow whisper.

The rumbling passed again, this time from the front of the U-Boat to the stern, and on the port side.

"Not unless we're caught in a crossfire…" whispered Kleiner, only half in reply.

The ship fell silent again. Krauser felt cold adrenaline flood his veins, and he suddenly felt sick to his stomach. "Maybe it hasn't noticed we're here. Maybe it can't find us when we're running silent," said Krauser.

Kleiner physically paled. "It? You mean…?"

Krauser nodded as the rumble once again came from stern to prow, and on the starboard side. "It's circling us. Trying to find us."

"What do we do?"

Krauser felt saturated with cold sweat. The adrenaline was making his entire body tingle with cold electricity. His brain kicked into overdrive, trying to think what to do. His mouth moved soundlessly before he eventually replied. "I don't know."

Sweat dripped off his forehead and down his back, but it felt like an ice flow this time. He had seen how fast the shark could lunge when it found food, not to mention Dahlen's description of the sheer force behind its bite. If it attacked while they were submerged, not a man would make it out alive. Yet, if silent running was the only camouflage they had against the foul sea monster, then an attempt to surface would be suicide.

Could they drive it off, somehow? Again, how could they do that without breaking silent running? Part of him wished that he had taken Dahlen's advice when he had the chance to. They could be up there on the surface, weapons prepared, and ready to carry out the fishing trip to end all fishing trips.

Instead, he had led them to a dark, cold silence, as good as any grave.

Again the shark passed down the port side and he could hear the gasps and whispers, curses and prayers from the men of the U-616. Krauser remained silent himself, desperate to do all he could to hide from the beast.

He counted the seconds in his head, and finally reached three hundred. "It's gone," he whispered.

"Are you sure?"

Krauser used the periscope once again. The freighter was now a mere four hundred metres away from them, and showed no sign of having noticed them. He spun the periscope a full circle, desperate to catch any sight of the shark, yet also hoping that it was long gone.

He turned back from the periscope and was surprised to see Dahlen standing behind him in the control room. There was something in the Norwegian man's eyes that indicated he was rattled, but the rest of his face was as stoic as ever. "I say we have no more doubts that this shark is hunting your boat."

Krauser looked around the control room, and saw that Kleiner and the other crew were watching him. He considered dismissing Dahlen's concerns with a show of bravado; but he knew that the time for that was long past. All the men had seen or felt or at least heard the stories of the colossal shark that haunted these waters, and to dismiss it out of hand would only serve to make him seem stupid, out of touch, or foolhardy. Instead he took in a breath, let it out steadily, and nodded. "Yes. This thing is hunting us, which is another reason why I am turning us back for home and safety before any more lives are lost."

"Captain, the *Freyr* could easily manage more than twice the speed of your boat, and this monster managed to catch it and tear it to pieces. You think that you can outrun it?"

"No, but I think we can outpace it. We can make seventeen knots on the surface, admittedly slower underwater, but still a good, constant speed. Even assuming that our fishy friend out there can swim faster than that, it will still have to stop to sleep. We can rotate crews and move constantly. The shark will tire, Mr Dahlen. The U-616 will not."

Dahlen nodded assent. "I hope you are right. However, I must warn you, Captain…you continue to underestimate this sh-"

The rumbling that heralded the approach of the shark returned suddenly, harder and faster than before. It practically howled up from the rear, up the starboard side, and barrelled past the command room. The submarine rattled and shuddered as the monster passed by so close and so fast, causing several men – including Krauser – to lose their footing and fall. Equipment and supplies tumbled from cabinets and storage units as the boat rocked calamitously on its axis. It took only two or three seconds for the shark to pass them, but its wake left them rocking and shouting.

When the U-616 eventually stabilised and the crew dusted themselves down and got to their feet, Kleiner rushed to the periscope to see if he could spot the monster. Krauser was still sat on the floor, gripping his right bicep – the ruckus had caused his gunshot wound to open up again, turning his shirt sleeve a deep red. Dahlen helped him to his feet and raised an eyebrow. "You are okay?"

"I will survive."

"You are still sure your boat can out pace this shark?"

Krauser shook his head and muttered. "I am not sure of anything anymore."

"Captain!" called Kleiner, from the periscope. "The shark has attacked the freighter! They are sinking!"

-TWELVE-

Krauser shakily made his way over to the periscope, gripping his bleeding arm. He peered through the viewfinder and saw that the freighter was indeed listing dangerously to one side. He muttered a curse under his breath. He knew that Dahlen would take this as some sort of twisted moral victory, claiming that the freighter had been sunk because of his refusal to stay and destroy the shark earlier. He was about to once again raise the notion that it could be a fellow U-Boat, or even a Wolf Pack operating in the area, when he saw the three metre high fin of the shark pass across his view, roughly halfway between them and the freighter. He jumped backwards and swore.

"What is it?" asked Kleiner. "Captain?"

"It's the shark," whispered Krauser. "It's attacked the freighter. Maintain silent running. Maybe it'll leave us alone and fill itself up on those sailors."

"What?" shouted Dahlen. "You cannot leave those men as a distraction, as bait, as *chum*! Are you Nazis really so divorced from your humanity that this is acceptable to you? Those are men, not some terrain to be taken advantage of."

Krauser nodded to an ensign. "Mr Letzer, please escort Mr Dahlen back to his bunk."

Dahlen shook off the ensign's hand as soon as it touched his arm. "I can find my own way back. Krauser, I hope you know what you're doing."

Krauser kept his face blank as the Norwegian was shown from the command room; though the truth be told, he was deeply shaken inside. He knew the effect of his actions – or rather, his inactions - but the fact was that his responsibility lay with his boat and his crew. Surely Dahlen had to understand that?

The command room seemed doubly silent following the outburst of a moment before, and it made the atmosphere turn even tenser, if such a thing were believable. Occasionally a shudder would run the length of the submarine as the shark swam by them; sometimes to port, sometimes to starboard and once, terrifyingly, directly underneath them. Kleiner maintained a watch on the periscope, and at least a quarter of an hour passed before he spoke. "I just saw its fin, sir. It's circling the freighter."

"Distance?"

"Six hundred...maybe seven hundred metres, sir."

"Any sign of lifeboats?"

Kleiner squinted and panned around a little. "No, sir. Do you think he...?"

Krauser nodded. "Surface."

The bells and klaxons and shouts of the crew heralded the surfacing of the U-616 like a hallelujah chorus. As soon as they were surfaced,

Krauser rushed up to the deck. Accompanied by Kleiner and the newly arrived Hertz, he felt his breath knocked from his chest as he saw the shark surface.

It swam up from the water in a lazy rolling action. At first all he saw was an explosion of white foam and spray, but then he saw the cavernous mouth, full of teeth like a foul warren made of bayonets. At a distance of three hundred metres he couldn't quite make out the one, glossy black eye, but he knew it was there, searching for them. Searching for the U-616.

As if running in slow motion, the fin emerged next, and Krauser saw that it was indeed fully three metres tall. It flexed slightly with the motion of the shark, and he could see places where it had been tattered and gouged over the years, in countless battles.

It occurred to him that he'd never really thought about how old the shark could be. It was no baby, for sure, but could it be twenty, thirty years old? Older? Had it been picking off merchant ships since the 1500s, the source for all sorts of legends of killer sea monsters for millennia?

Could it be older than that? Could it have feasted on dinosaur flesh?

Could it...could it be a dinosaur itself? Some relic from the cretaceous era that had somehow survived the apocalypse of all its kind?

Then, time seemed to rush to catch up with its momentary delay as, for the first time,the muscular, ghost grey length of its body rolled up from the depths. Krauser gasped as it soared through the surf; it had to be twenty five, even thirty metres in length, dwarfing that of the largest Great Whites he had ever heard tell of. Dinosaur, sea monster, mutation…that did not seem to matter. What mattered was that this thing was alive, hungry, and coming for them.

"The goddamn thing is heading straight for us!" shouted Hertz. "Captain, we have to move!"

Krauser was frozen as the shark barrelled straight for their submarine, travelling at an ungodly speed.

Hertz grabbed him by the arm and pulled him, almost threw him, towards the hatch to the command room. "Captain! We have to move!"

Krauser nodded, as if in a dream and had slid down the ladder into the command room before he realised what he was doing. "Turn this boat around, one hundred and eighty degrees, and get us out of here at once. Full speed!"

A chorus of ayes and acknowledgments answered him, and he felt the diesel engines kick into life, as if the ship had been holding steady, like a car in gear, waiting for his command to drop the handbrake. Kleiner and Hertz slid down the ladder quickly after him, grabbing hold of rungs or pipes to stop themselves from falling as the U-616 began a rapid turn from a dead stop.

"Did you see what it was doing?" demanded Krauser. "Is it still heading straight for us?"

"It dove!" Kleiner shouted over the roar of the engines. The command room seemed impossibly noisy after the silent running of the previous half an hour or so. "It dropped out of sight about a hundred and fifty metres out from us, and then Hertz and I followed you down here. Captain…what are we going to do?"

"We're getting the hell out of here, Mr Kleiner. I'm not going to end up as fish food, and neither are you. And that's an order."

"Aye aye, Captain."

The engineer turned to continue his work, and Krauser addressed his second in command. "Mr Hertz?"

"Captain."

"Thank you for your assistance up on deck."

"Don't mention it, Captain."

"You're a good man, Mr Hertz. I'll be putting in a letter of commendation and recommendation for your promotion when we return to shore."

Suddenly, they were thrown violently around as a grating shudder heralded the shark passing directly beneath them. Only their grip on struts, rungs and pipes prevented them from being thrown to the floor. "I think you mean *if* we return to shore, sir."

"Maintain full speed. We can outpace this thing." He looked down at his sleeve, turned crimson from the reopened bullet wound. "Take charge, Mr Hertz. I need to report to Dr Arnold."

***

Krauser was having his wound stitched when Arnild Dahlen approached them. "Captain. I would like to apologise for what happened on the bridge earlier. I let my emotions get the better of me. I understand why you are doing what you are doing. I am sorry."

Krauser smiled, then hissed in pain as the doctor re-stitched his wound. "Apology accepted, Mr Dahlen."

They both froze as another rumble, like an underground train passing on the next platform heralded another sweeping pass of the shark. They all looked up, despite it clearly being on the starboard side, and Krauser remembered the depth charges. A few seconds passed before conversation continued.

"I don't know how we could hunt a shark anyway," said the doctor. "We have torpedoes and the deck gun and anti-aircraft, for sure, but those are all best suited to static or slow moving targets at range. I dare say there wouldn't be time for us to aim or calibrate the weapons. The shark would be on us before we knew it."

"I've arranged for some men to stand watch up top, and given them what weapons we could find," said Krauser.

"What do they have?" asked Dahlen, his stoic tone returned.

"Not much."

***

Ensigns Sessler and Gerstner stood up on the deck, keeping watch for the monster that followed them. They had been kitted out with the finest weapons the captain could find them – Sessler held a revolver, and Gerstner the largest meat cleaver from the kitchen, neither of which filled them with any degree of security or confidence. Sessler watched the fore and starboard of the boat, Gerstner the aft and port. If they spotted anything, they were to shout down into the command room where they had seen it, so that the control room crew could decide which way to steer and what to do.

"You see anything?" asked Sessler, lighting a cigarette. He was in his mid-twenties, dark and tall.

Gertner was a much younger man, fair haired and small. Many suspected he was fifteen or sixteen, and had lied about his age to join up with the Kriegsmarine. "Nothing. How the hell are we supposed to see anything up here anyway?"

"It's just a shark. I don't even know why we're running."

"The Captain says it's big."

"Oh, please. How big can it be?"

-THIRTEEN-

The boat rocked sharply, tilting on its axis, throwing the entire crew almost forty-five degrees to starboard. Instantly, all aboard knew what had attacked them.

Krauser heard Sessler and Gerstner's screams from the control room and kicked into action straight away. Grabbing his Mauser, he darted for the ladder up to the deck, climbing it in seconds. The sunlight and salt spray momentarily dazzled him when he emerged on deck, but he noticed the ungodly stench instantly. The smell of fish guts and the iron tinged stench of blood hit him like a brick wall. When at last his eyes adjusted to the brightness and he took in his surroundings, he saw Sessler – certainly dead - torn in half on the deck. Below the rib cage he was no more than a mess of strands of viscera and shards of bone. The screaming came from Gerstner, who was kneeling by the dead man, chewing his fist and rocking back and forth. Sessler's blood, thinned by the sea water, was spreading around them both.

Krauser ran to Gerstner and squatted beside him, gripping his shoulders. "Which side did it come from? Did you see it?"

"It…it just…it rose up. I couldn't do anything. There was a noise…I thought it was an explosion…then it was just…there. He fell…he slid to it…and it…"

The captain pulled the man up and almost threw him toward the entrance hatch. "Go. Get below."

Sessler slid down the ladder, still gibbering to himself. Krauser was hot on his heels and about to follow when he heard a sound like a thunderclap, and felt the cold water wash over him. The deck tilted under his feet, and he had to grab hold of the barrel of the anti-aircraft gun to stand upright. He blinked, wiped the water from his eyes with his sleeve, and turned to face the shark.

It was once again, attempting to climb up the side of the boat, tugging it on its axis. The jaws worked desperately trying to reach him, the teeth made even more horrific now by the pieces of Sessler and his uniform ground into paste between them. The leviathan made involuntary deep barking noises as it reached for him, oddly putting him in mind of the sighs and grunts of an old dog he had known on the farm he grew up on. Krauser wrapped one arm around a fixing, gripping it in his elbow, so that he could take his automatic pistol in both hands and fire precisely.

The shark thrashed and shifted around, emitting its odd, breathy barking, and Krauser had the sense that the shark was looking for him with its one good eye. He took aim, and squeezed off three rounds in fast but smooth succession.

He was rewarded by small puffs of red mist where the bullets struck the beast, but they made no impact on it. The shark thrashed, causing the deck to shake under his feet once more, pulling it forty-five degrees towards it, and he skidded on the sodden wood. He lost his grip on the strut and fell hard onto his backside, cracking his tailbone. He screamed as he slid down towards the vast, foetid maw, and knew his time had come. The deck was a ramp to death.

He screamed, took aim, and fired off three more shots from the Mauser, satisfaction of a sort filling him to see two of them strike it full on in the teeth, shattering bone. He was a mere two feet from the thing's mouth when he stopped suddenly, his jacket caught on something.

"Captain!" shouted Hertz, who had caught hold of the collar of his jacket. "Get below now!"

Krauser was so close he could physically feel the air being pushed around by the monster's desperate bites. He threw his pistol at the shark, watching it bounce harmlessly off the thing's nose. With his hands now free he was able to get a grip on the planks of the deck and clamber backwards towards the hatch, Hertz desperately tugging him along all the while. At last he reached the hatch, and he felt himself pulled backwards through the bulkhead, both of them skidding down the ladder together. The boat rocked rapidly, righting itself as the shark disengaged the attack and swam off.

Krauser and Hertz lay panting together for a while, until some of the men came to their aid and helped them to their feet.

"Thank you, Mr Hertz. I would have died if not for you."

Hertz breathlessly snapped a salute. "It was nothing. That was very brave of you to rescue Gerstner, not to mention launch a full on attack on the shark."

Krauser doubled over, struggling to get his breath back, and suppressed the urge to vomit. "Where has it gone? What do we do?"

Hertz took Krauser by the arm, his eyes manic. "Captain…I have to say that I agree with our Norwegian friend. We have to kill this thing, and we have to kill it now. If we don't then who knows wh-"

The shark took its opportunity when it could. Now charging the submarine directly side on from its starboard, it gripped the submarine in its jaws and wrenched it as hard as it could. The U-616 was rocked and thrown side to side and tossed in its jaws like a dog with a toy. Men screamed as they were suddenly thrown up, down and sideways in rapid succession. The monster's teeth ground down hard and the hull screamed as if in pain.

At last the shark loosened its bite and the boat skidded sideways in the water.

There was a distant scream of metal, and a jet of sea water pulsed into the control room!

"Breach!" screamed Kleiner, who hurried towards it with another engineer to assess the damage.

"Torpedo loose!" came several screams along the length of the boat.

Bells rung and men shouted. Krauser's head rang. He put his hand to his forehead and it came away slick with blood. His vision swam. He supposed that this was how it had to end. His last thoughts were of his wife and unborn child.

Dahlen splashed through the ankle deep water in the control room and pulled Hertz to his feet. "What do we do now?"

"I...I don't know. If this were a depth charge or a bombing run, I'd give the order to submerge, but there is nothing we can do. The attack comes from below the sea."

Dahlen shivered in the cold water and pulled Krauser up, throwing the captain's arm over his shoulder to carry him out. "That is a bad head wound. We need to get him to the doctor."

Hertz slid under Krauser's other arm to aid him. He shouted for the men to clear the way as they hurried to Dr Arnold's station.

"What would you do if we were being attacked by another submarine? Surely that is the same principle?"

They fell sideways as the shark rammed them again. The hull physically buckled around them, and Dahlen caught a gush of sea water directly in the face. Hertz alerted the men to the new breach and continued carrying the captain to the doctor. "It's not the same principle at all. Submarines are almost stationary when they attack. This monster is faster than we are. It can attack from all angles. It can smash us at close range. At close range all we have are knives and small arms fire."

They burst into the doctor's station as the boat lurched sickeningly one more time. They kept their feet this time, but heard the bursting of steam pipes and screams of "Fire! Fire!" from the engine room.

Dr Arnold was as white as a sheet. "What in god's name is happening? Is it an airstrike?"

"Shark attack, Dr Arnold," replied Dahlen.

"Shark? Your shark?"

"Our shark." He grunted, throwing Krauser onto a bed. "Is he dead?"

Dr Arnold began a rapid examination of the captain. "No, not dead. Unconscious, though. Probably a concussion. He'll need to rest up for some time. Leave him with me. Mr Hertz, you're in command until such time as I deem our captain fit for duty."

"I know that, doctor. Please, do all you can for…wait…"

"What is it?" asked Dahlen, getting his breath back from the laborious rush to the doctor's station.

"It's stopped," replied Hertz.

The doctor and Dahlen turned their eyes skyward, listening. A minute passed, then two.

"You're right," said the doctor, tying off a bandage he had quickly applied to Krauser's head. "Does this mean we're safe?"

"No, doctor," said Dahlen. "It just means that the shark is resting. Predators sometimes like to injure their prey, so that it tires itself out and they can follow it at their leisure, rather than expend all their energy in an all-out attack. Perhaps sharks do the same. It's certainly how it brought down the *Freyr*."

Hertz nodded. "He's right. What it means is that we have to take advantage of this time to repair our boat and prepare as many offensive capabilities as we can. Knives, guns, explosives, anything. We have to kill this thing before it kills us."

***

Captain Krauser's eyes flickered open. He couldn't quite focus on the room around him, and when he went to raise himself up on his elbows, a friendly hand pushed him down again.

"You took a bump to the head, Captain," came the familiar voice of Dr Arnold. "Hertz and Dahlen brought you here. How are you feeling?"

"Like I have a *katzenjammer*."

Dr Arnold chuckled. "How is your vision?"

"Foggy. Like I can't quite focus. It blurs and then refocuses, blurs and refocuses."

"I suspect you have a concussion. You need to rest. Johann Hertz has taken command for the moment."

Krauser forcefully got himself out of bed, and shook his head lightly. "I'm sorry doctor, but I cannot leave my men now. I have to go find Hertz and get a damage report."

Arnold shrugged. "I suspect it will do no harm. Not now."

Krauser paused at the door, surprised to see the doctor so downbeat. "What do you mean?"

"Captain, the U-616 is sinking."

-FOURTEEN-

Krauser staggered his way through the cramped corridors of the submarine, buffeted by the men and assaulted by the heat. He finally made his way to the control room and walked directly into Hertz, stumbling back a step or two. The second in command caught him before he fell and steadied him. "Captain Krauser? I was not expecting you back on duty so soon."

Krauser blinked away the bleariness from his eyes. "Neither was I, but I don't think this is a time that any of us can afford to spend resting. What are we dealing with?"

"Captain, the situation is exceedingly dire. The hydroplanes are stuck, and one of them has even been sheared off completely. We can't submerge; and even if we did, we couldn't surface again."

Krauser swore. "That's the last thing we need. That White Ghost is coming back, we have no weapons, and we can't hide should a plane or a destroyer happen to chance upon us."

"White Ghost?"

The Captain shrugged. "Just a name that came to me for it. It's so old it's not really grey anymore, you know? It looks faded and wraith like. It's as if all the dead of the ocean had come together to make a ghost."

Hertz raised an eyebrow.

"Cut me some slack, I've hit my head pretty hard. It doesn't matter, anyway. So, we have no weapons and no way of hiding should we need to?"

The older man nodded. "I've been talking to the men. We've been preparing a line of defence against the…White Ghost…and I'll come to that in a moment. It's just that there's something more than the hydroplanes, sir."

Krauser braced himself. What could possibly be worse than the hydroplanes? "Go on."

"The hull is cracked down the port side. We're taking in a lot of water. I've got the men working the pumps to try and bail us out but…it's not going to work for long, sir."

Krauser sighed and nodded. "How fast can we go?"

"I'd estimate we're limping along at around five to seven knots, sir."

Krauser pulled a cigarette from his pocket and headed to the ladder. "Come join me on deck."

Simply getting out of the dark humidity of the submarine and standing up on the deck seemed to help in blowing the cobwebs from his brain. His vision still pulsed strangely every now and again like a bad hangover, but it was starting to fade. The deck was listing at a slight angle – not enough to make you lose your footing, but once you noticed it, it became impossible to ignore. Some of the men were attempting minor repairs to the anti-aircraft gun and some surface damage. After a couple of drags on his cigarette, he noticed Dahlen. The Norwegian man was sat cross legged by the deck gun, working on something in his lap.

Dahlen didn't notice Krauser and Hertz approaching, and it was only when Krauser gave him a playful nudge with his boot that he looked up. "Captain!" he smiled, "It is very good to see you up and about! How are you feeling?"

Krauser smiled back. "I've been better, but I am better than I was when I first woke, thank you. What is that you are working on, my friend?"

Dahlen clambered to his feet, and the two Germans saw that he was holding a length of steel pipe, about two metres long, around the end of which he had lashed a serrated knife that he had obviously looted from the kitchen. "Mr Hertz here said that there was a lack of weapons with which to fight off our shark. So, I improvised."

Krauser laughed. "I must say that I like your thinking, Mr Dahlen. Torpedoes and anti-aircraft weapons will do us no good, so here we must fight like our ancestors. Fishing with sticks and stones!"

Dahlen did not laugh and simply handed the makeshift spear to the U-Boat captain. "Yes. Like our ancestors. Your ancestors destroyed the Roman Empire – the greatest empire the world has ever seen, and far greater than I fear your Mister Hitler will accomplish. And mine? Mine were the Vikings, who plundered and massacred their way across the known world and beyond. Tell me,

Captain and Mr Hertz. Can the descendants of Vikings and Goths stand up to one little sea monster? I say we can, even if it be *Jörmungandr* himself!"

Krauser was amused, and a little stirred by the man's brief speech. He was right. They were in these waters because they were warriors of their people and they would not be brought low by a mere fish! He accepted the spear graciously. Dahlen handed one more to Hertz, and held the third for himself.

Hertz smiled wryly. "I think I still have faith in the deck gun, Mr Dahlen."

Dahlen chuckled and hefted his spear. "I think we shall have to use whatever weapons are available to us."

The three men turned quickly at a shout from the other side of the deck. It took them a moment to realise what was happening, as three of the crew jumped up and down, pointing and screaming ceaselessly.

"It's back…" breathed Krauser. "This is the last time, friends."

About five or six hundred metres out, a wake was visible in the water, and speeding towards them rapidly.

"It's a torpedo…" whispered Hertz.

"Mr Hertz, do you really believe that yourself?" asked Dahlen, banging the butt of his spear on the deck and advancing towards the crew.

***

Five hundred metres out from U-616, the monster bore down upon its prey as it had done since birth. It was their shark. It was Krauser's White Ghost and Dahlen's *Jörmungandr*. To the sailors that had come before them, it was The Sea Monster. It was The Kraken. It was Carcharocles Megalodon. In its time it had sunk boats of steel, and galleons of wood. It had taken men in uniform, and it had taken men in furs. It had taken dolphin, walrus, shark and whale, in equal measure.

It hunted the submarine the same as it had hunted its prey for unmeasured years. It would debilitate, first of all - crushing the soft appendages - and then delivering a crushing blow to the ribcage of its prey. There its teeth would crush and rend and maul the organs within. The fish – be it metal or wood or meat – would flail and it would flounder and it would be consumed.

The shark had suffered many wounds, and it knew that it would suffer many more. Many years past, another sea monster - all scales and teeth, the spirit of a crocodile with the shape of an eel – had taken a chunk from its tail. A brave human, clad in bronze armor and a red crested helmet, had taken its eye with its spear. Both the sea monster and the brave human had been consumed eventually, and since then it had learned to take its time with any prey.

The boat had been chased for long enough now. He had taken some of its soldiers. He had cracked the puny fish's dorsal fins, and smashed its ribs with its mammoth jaws.

It was – at last – time to feed.

-FIFTEEN-

Time seemed to slow down for Krauser, as he watched the Norwegian reach the crew. Dahlen pulled the men back and shoved them behind him, urging them to head towards the entrance hatch. The men staggered and stumbled away from the approaching shark, but Dahlen stood ready, his spear gripped in two hands, pointed towards his enemy. The wake of the shark came closer - two hundred metres, one fifty – until suddenly it sank from view.

Krauser ran over to his friend, and grabbed his arm. "It's submerged. It means to attack us from below once more!"

Dahlen shook his head. "No. I have seen it do this before."

"What do you mean?"

There was a deafening thunderclap, and Krauser felt the spray of the sea on him, as he turned to the source of the noise.

The shark – his White Ghost – had leapt out of the water in a vicious lunge towards them. It hadn't entirely cleared the water, but he saw enough of it to finally truly appreciate its size. It wasn't just huge, for "huge" was not the right word: it was colossal, gargantuan, even. It was not a shark so much as a prehistoric creature of nightmares taken the form of a hideous, stocky, scarred Great White. The leviathan's one working black eye took in the U-616 dispassionately, and it landed on the deck with another thunderclap. Krauser lost his footing, went down hard on his backside, and found himself skidding and sliding towards the water. No! Not towards the water! Towards the mouth of the monster that had beached itself on his submarine!

The deck listed at a hard angle as the weight of the monster attempted to drag it under. Krauser managed to steady himself by grabbing a railing, but some of the crew were not so lucky. Two fell directly into the sea, and a third tumbled straight into the maw of the megalodon. His screams changed sharply in pitch from fear to agony as he fell side on into the teeth that then clamped down hard. When the mouth next opened, the man had been almost entirely bisected, held together by just his spine and several stringy pieces of gristle. Krauser vomited, and desperately tried to stand upright, using his spear as a makeshift crutch.

Dahlen let out a deadly war cry and thrust his knife tipped spear into the shark's mouth. The knife sank deep into the gum line, causing a spurt of red blood to flow and mingle with the dead sailor's. Twice, then thrice more he jabbed into the roof of the monster's mouth. The shark exhaled a low grunt that stank like a fishmonger's on a hot day, lifted its head up, and then sharply down again, crashing onto the submarine with all its weight. The submarine shuddered in the water, and tilted at an increasingly terrifying angle. Maintaining their footing was proving harder and harder for all of them.

The Norwegian had fallen onto his backside, and only managed to get back up again with Hertz's assistance. Hertz had drawn his revolver and was pumping shot after shot into the shark's face. The rocking of the boat and his nerves threw his aim off, however, and only one of the rounds hit, just above the thing's eye, and they were rewarded with the sight of a chunk of flesh flying off.

Krauser yelled as they sensed the thing's pain. He thought it exceptionally unlikely that they would be able to kill this thing, but if they hurt it enough, it was just possible that it could be driven off, in search of much easier prey. If they could persuade it to go off in search of an easier meal, they could make it out of here alive! He stepped back two paces and launched his knife-spear like a javelin. It arced high, and sank in by the massive dorsal fin. It had lodged in! He laughed loudly, and shouted his victory to Hertz and Dahlen. Dahlen launched his own, but his aim went much too high and the spear splashed into the water behind the shark.

Hertz threw his own spear to Krauser, urging him to take another shot, before turning to Dahlen. "Come with me. I have another idea."

The shark thrashed left and right, in search of its attackers, and once again Krauser was forced to grab hold of a railing for stability. The shark headbutted up and down again, shaking the deck once more. Fearing for his life, Krauser screamed and threw his spear hard at the monster's face. The knife point entered the jaw and knocked a tooth loose – but what was one tooth from that hell hole of death and destruction? The spear clattered sideways, and fell into the ocean.

The monster belched another gust of foul stench and had Krauser not already emptied his stomach he would have done so then. The creature's breath stank of all the pain and misery this thing had ever caused. It was the gust of death from the Mariana Trench. It was beyond foulness.

Just as he prepared himself for the White Ghost to launch itself against him, it let out a sighing burp and slid back and into the ocean. The waves passed over it, and but for the death and destruction in its wake, it was as if it had never been there. Krauser shivered and shook with shock, hearing the blood rushing around his body, and feeling every ache and pain in his muscles (especially the bullet wound which had begun to throb once more). He felt partially deafened, as though his head had been held under ice cold water. Eventually, this feeling began to subside, and he heard his name called from across the deck.

With what felt like an Olympic effort, he raised his head and turned to the deck gun, where Hertz and Dahlen had it ready to fire. Yes! He jogged across the slippery deck to his friends, and laughed. "Yes! Yes, this could work."

Hertz nodded. "I think so, Captain. We just need...well, we just need a little bait."

Dahlen hopped down from the firing seat and shook some water from his hair. "While you were down there earlier, Hertz and I did a dry run. I think we can actually hit it. Our bullets and knives are wounding it, but not deeply or severely enough. I think an eighty-eight millimetre shell might make a touch of difference, though."

Krauser shivered. "So, you need me back there as bait?"

"No. I will go. It is yours and Hertz's boat, and it is your gun. You should be the ones to kill this thing. My place is down in the front."

"That's lunacy!"

"It is not more lunacy than any of this, Captain. This shark has had ten chances or more to eat me; I do not think that this time will make any difference to my odds in the long run."

The Norwegian man pulled a kitchen cleaver from his belt, and turned to go, when the captain called after him.

"Arild...be safe."

"I will. You too, August."

Hertz had hopped gleefully into the firing position. "Standing ready, Captain."

Dahlen strode to the far end of the deck and, showing no signs of fear or disgust, picked up a hunk of half-chewed sailor and threw it into the ocean before stamping in the shallow waters a few times, shouting a challenge to the shark that hunted them.

"Do you think it'll come?" asked Hertz.

"It'll come. It'll keep coming until we're dead," replied Krauser, coldly.

The deck suddenly shook beneath their feet, as the shark rose up from the port side. Dahlen screamed and ran towards it, ducking in and back again, swinging with his cleaver when he felt brave enough, though the blade was old and seemed to do little damage.

"Aim the deck gun, Mr Hertz!" shouted Krauser, above the clamour and cries of the battling Viking and sea monster. The deck gun slowly, painfully slowly, cranked into position and his brave second-in-command positioned the gun as best as he could. He was a commander of men, not a hands-on gunner; and although he knew the theory behind the attack, the theory he had learned did not extend to close quarters fighting with demon sharks.

"Ready?" shouted Krauser.

"Ready!"

"Take aim!"

"Aimed!"

"F-"

The shark jumped higher out of the water, lunging an extra six feet or so towards Dahlen. The Norwegian was taken by surprise and while he managed to avoid being caught in the monster's jaws, he was caught full on by the side of its head. He fell hard on his back, the cleaver skittering away, and struck his head hard on the deck. Krauser screamed as he saw the man slide down the length of the deck to the stern, and into the cold, deadly water of the North Sea, disappearing with an ominous splash.

The shark seemed to smile cruelly, before sliding back off of the deck, and going in search of its prize.

Krauser screamed after it, but this had even less effect than the bullets had.

The U-616 was almost capsized in the water, their weapons were all useless, his men were dying, and the shark was still hungry.

-SIXTEEN-

Krauser acted without thinking, and ran across and down the tilting deck, diving into the water after Dahlen. Hertz screamed after him to stop, but he had never listened to the man before, so why should he start now? He just knew that it didn't seem fair that Dahlen should perish this time; not when he had been through and survived so much. How could he have survived the sinking of the *Freyr*, and his own lifeboat, only to die now?

The shock of entering the ice cold water hit him like a punch to the chest. He felt his whole body momentarily seize up, and stiffen – refusing even to breathe or for his eyes to blink or his heart to beat. After this half a second long nightmare, he recovered a little, and ducked under the water, eyes wide open, desperate to see a sign of Dahlen.

What he saw instead, a mere six feet away from him, was his White Ghost.

It had to be at least thirty metres long, and it swam oh so slowly past him. He had to fight desperately to suppress a sob of pure terror as this antediluvian nightmare, this vile cousin of the Great White, slowly passed him in the dark blue of the ocean. He felt the motion as it pushed its bulk through the water and was buffeted in the underwater crosswinds of its passing.

It was the agonising slowness of its passing that got to him. The shark was not trying to fight him. The shark was not trying to chase him. The shark was not even trying to avoid him. He was insignificant to it. It did not fear him, hate him, want him or desire him. He was nothing to this creature that had patrolled these waters for god only knows how long or how far. He became aware of how small humanity was in the grand scheme of the history of the planet, and how little he meant even to that. He remembered thinking earlier in his bunk that in the grand scheme of the war he was merely an ash on the fire that consumed the world. In truth, the fire that consumed the world was no more than a spark – no, an ember – on the rock of history.

Alone, unarmed, bobbing in the ice cold waters of the North Sea, he was on the verge of tears.

When, after what seemed a lifetime, the tattered, scarred tail of the thing swam past his eyes, Krauser desperately came to the surface for air, gasping in two deep lungfuls of it, before quickly ducking under in search of Dahlen.

***

Johann Hertz skidded down the ladder into the control room, almost falling directly on top of Kleiner. Grabbing the engineer by the shirt, he screamed. "Are the ballast tanks functional?"

Kleiner went white under the mad glare of the officer. "What? Sir, that's…that's lunacy! You want us to go deeper into the water? With that thing? Sir, it'll destroy us!"

"I don't want us to dive. I want us to blow all the water out of the ballast tanks. Even if they're empty, blow them again. I want to keep this boat as upright as possible. I'm taking command."

"Captain Krauser?"

"Captain Krauser fell into the ocean with that thing." Hertz paused and smiled. "I am in command of the U-616 now, Engineer Kleiner, and I want this boat ready and upright. That thing's going to come in for another run at us, and when it does, I want to fire all torpedoes, and the deck gun. I don't care how big and tough it is, it's not big and tough enough to survive a salvo from the U-616."

"Yes, sir. I'll give the order right away," muttered Kleiner, shaken by the news of the death of his captain.

Hertz dismissed the man and issued another order. "I want all forwards torpedo tubes locked and loaded. I'm going up top. I need two men with me. As soon as we catch sight of where that thing is, I want us taking aim and getting ready to blow it back to the Pleistocene Era."

***

The surviving crew of the U-616 ran, carrying out Hertz's order as quickly as possible. The news of Captain August Krauser's death spread quickly, and some tears were shed, though they did not pause to grieve. They had a job to do, and the time to remember the good captain would come later.

The crew working the pumps moved at double time, cranking and pumping harder and faster than ever before, until they actually convinced themselves that they could feel the boat rising from the water; that they could – yes – they could feel the U-616 righting itself on its axis, so that it was as ready as it had ever been!

They convinced themselves that there was only one God given Hunter of the North Sea, and that it was the Kriegsmarine!

***

Hertz was startled in the control room by Dr Arnold. "Captain?"

"Yes, Doctor. What can I do for you?"

"I want to help. I have made all the injured as comfortable as possible, but I am now growing restless. I'm not an engineer, but…there must be something I can do."

"Yes. Do you own binoculars?"

The doctor was more than a little unnerved by the wide-eyed and manic stare of the Lieutenant Hertz, but knew better than to say anything. "Yes, I'm certain I can rustle up a pair."

Hertz turned from him and continued reloading his revolver. "Good. Head up onto the deck when you have a pair. I'll need as many eyes on the ocean as I can get. I'm heading up now, myself."

Dr Arnold dashed off to find his binoculars, as Hertz clambered up onto the deck.

Hertz was amazed how much damage the shark had managed to do. Struts and railings were mangled and destroyed. Tooth indentations marred the length of the hull as it had tried to chew its way in to the submarine. He supposed that to the shark, the U-616 was just an especially belligerent shellfish. He posted one man to the aft, one to port and one to starboard and – when he arrived – the good doctor to the fore. Hertz himself stood by the deck gun, doing his best to look in all directions. He had three men ready and working the deck gun, knowing that should the shark approach from the sides, this would be their only means of defence.

***

Krauser was having to swim further and further from the U-616. Now he was far and away to the rear of the boat, and had lost all hope of ever finding Dahlen – his friend had to be either drowned or eaten. He was keen to get back to his submarine – and likely to wrestle command back from Hertz – but every time he had tried to swim back, he had ended up exhausted, struggling against a strong current – or he had had to freeze to avoid running directly into the shark again. He had read somewhere that sharks are able to hunt their prey by the motions they made while swimming, and he had no reason to suppose that this monster hunted by any other method.

Once he had actually felt the thing graze against him, and was sure that he had been detected. Its skin had felt rough, like a cat's tongue, and covered with lumpy, bulbous scar tissue. What little damage they had caused the thing earlier with Dahlen's makeshift spears seemed to have been shrugged off already. There was no sign of injury to the monster.

When next he surfaced for air, he took the time to look all around him, and was surprised to see something on the horizon. It could have been a mile away or more, but it looked to him like…yes, it was a boat! He didn't know if they were friendly, or neutral or enemy, but he knew that he had a better chance of making it to them, than he did to the submarine. Could he abandon his ship and his men? What would his wife think? The Kriegsmarine?

His wife would want him home and safe, and he knew that the cold, hard Kriegsmarine would rather have a captain alive than dead. He could always be assigned to a new U-Boat; you couldn't assign a boat to a dead captain.

Once again his head and his heart were at war.

***

"Lieutenant Hertz!" shouted the doctor, dropping his binoculars to the deck with a clatter, and running over to the gun, waving.

Hertz signalled to Kleiner and the deck gun crew to prepare themselves and caught the doctor as the panicked man fell to his knees. "What is it, doctor? Have you seen it?"

Dr Arnold was a wreck, his eyes were as wide as saucers and his finger jabbed sharply in the direction he had just run from. He was sweating and near tears in seconds. "It's...it's there...huge...we have to get out of here!"

Hertz pulled up his own binoculars and looked to where the panicked doctor was pointing. It was true. The shark's fin had broken up through the water, about eight hundred metres from the front of the U-616. He shouted orders to the deck gun to get their bearing.

Dr Arnold was clawing at Hertz's trouser leg weeping. "We have to get out of here! Abandon ship! It's a monster! They said it was a big shark but I just thought it was a big shark, not this! This is a goddamn... a dinosaur! We have to get out of here! Now!"

"Dr Arnold get yourself below deck, or come to your senses. We have a fish to catch."

"No! No! We have to run! We have to get out of here now! Don't you see? It's a monster! A goddamn dinos-"

The men working deck gun paused at the crack of Acting Captain Johann Hertz shooting the doctor in the head, but returned to their work quickly, for fear that they would be next.

-SEVENTEEN-

Hertz shouted down the ladder into the control room to fire both torpedoes from the functioning fore tubes in rapid succession. There was, of course, the estimated dud ratio, but what little chance did he have? Even assuming the fifty percent dud ration that Captain Krauser had sworn by, he felt sure at least one of the torpedoes would catch the Megalodon and obliterate it into a stinking pulp.

The order was rapidly carried up the length of the U-Boat to the men working the torpedo tubes. The bulkheads were sealed, the torpedoes primed, safety checks carried out, and – finally – the first torpedo was spat forth from the submarine. The second followed in rapid succession, and Hertz watched the approaching shark through his binoculars, hoping to get a close view of the death and destruction that he - a true Kriegsmarine commander – had wrought.

***

The shark was not stupid. It hadn't managed to live to its age by being stupid. It had felt the push and ripple of the water that indicated something was travelling towards it, and pretty fast, too. In its time it had known other metal fish project similar attacks. It had once had his ribs painfully smashed by a wooden fish that had propelled a heavy metal ball fast and hard into his side. It had been overconfident, certain it was the hunter of the ocean and indestructible. Since then, it had learned to trust his instincts, and avoid these sort of attacks.

It was still confident it was the hunter of the ocean, however.

The shark pushed its nose downwards and dove, letting the torpedo swim harmlessly overhead.

It felt another pass soundless above it, and resurfaced, its fin breaking the water once more.

***

Hertz swore up a blue blaze as he saw the shark's fin resurface, this time a mere three hundred metres away. He screamed for the men to bring the deck gun to bear. Cranks were turned and wheels spun and the eighty-eight millimetre cannon focused on its target.

"Fire!" screamed the acting captain. He quickly slapped his hands to his ears as a large tank cannon round fired into the water where the shark had to be. Time slowed down and he thought he could hear a metallic zipping sound as the shell passed by in close proximity, followed by a hollow, bass splash as it thudded into the water.

The explosion in the water seemed cataclysmic. The shock wave pushed a large gout of water into the air and – could it be? – yes, it was tinged with red! Hertz fell to his knees laughing with pure unbridled triumph as pulpy red fish meat rained down on the deck. It was over! The deck gun had destroyed the monstrous shark!

He staggered to his feet, skidding slightly in the gore strewn across the wooden deck, and hurried to the men working the deck gun. They were just as jubilant as he, throwing their hats into the air, laughing and hugging one another. Hertz joined them in the handshakes, which rapidly evolved into hugs and backslaps. The U-616 had survived an engagement with an enemy like no other.

"Men, I think we owe it to ourselves to crack out the rum, don't you? Feininger, Spahn, go tell the crew. Tonight we celebrate!"

The rum was hurried up to the men on deck, and Hertz gave them a short speech, singing their praises and toasting their bravery. In truth, Kleiner and the men would rather have been downstairs; the compliments heaped upon them by a man they didn't really like or respect made them uncomfortable, and the deck was cold and stank of fishguts. Spahn lit a cigarette, hoping to give an impression of disrespect to their ersatz captain, but Hertz was enjoying the sound of his own voice so much that he didn't notice.

Hertz raised his glass for the final toast. "And, of course, it would be criminal of me not to mention the men we have lost along the way, though none are missed more so than our dear Captain August Krauser, who was a true hero of the Kriegsmarine. It's not easy taking over the job of captain in these circumstances, but I do hope that I am able t-"

The deck rocked sharply, and Hertz crashed hard flat onto his back, and skidded down the deck towards the now sinking prow of the boat. He span as he slid and fell and saw the meatgrinder maw of the megalodon waiting for him. It had survived! He saw that where its right fin had been was now a gaping, bleeding wound of viscera and cartilage, but the thing still lived.

Wide-eyed and screaming, Hertz scrambled and grasped for every handhold that he could get, but his fingers simply skittered uselessly over the damp wood of the deck. He shouted for help as his foot reached the creature's mouth up to the ankle; his scream then became wordless as the monster's jaw clamped down, driving nine inch serrated knives into him, crushing cartilage and bone. He looked down and saw the lump of mangled skeleton and pulpy flesh where his foot had once been, before the shark thrashed its head, pulling him further into its maw. Up to the waist this time, the thing bit down again and he felt each tooth stab into him like the knives of a hundred murderers. Organs ripped, flesh parted and he gasped as he felt his lungs and stomach fill with blood. He coughed up a spray of crimson before the shark undulated once more, and he felt himself sliding further in, and then he knew no more.

***

Grabbing hold of a shattered length of railing, Captain Krauser hauled himself up on deck, with a shout of rage and fear. He ran at full speed straight over to the deck gun, desperate to assist Kleiner and Spahn in reloading it for another shot. The shark, satisfied for the moment with its appetiser of Johann Hertz, slid off the deck and swam deep into the water.

A round from the deck gun thudded into the water where they figured the shark could likely be, but in his heart he knew that if he couldn't see it, then it could be anywhere.

Then, the fin broke up out of the water again, about five hundred metres out, in front of the submarine's prow.

Chief engineer Kleiner, struck by a sudden idea, abandoned the deck gun and ran to the ladder down to the control room. He screamed for the crew to load and fire torpedoes, but none could hear him. They were all desperately trying to right the craft, pump the water out of the ballast tanks and sustain their lives for another few minutes. He resolved to take matters into his own hands and skinned down the ladder and raced for the torpedo bay.

As he cannonballed down the narrow corridor, he was buffeted by panicked sailors, sprayed with gouts of water from the cracked hull and broiled alive by sweat and humidity of that undersea hell.

***

Krauser and Spahn were left manning the deck gun, and found themselves desperately struggling to get it loaded and into a position to fire. They knew that they didn't have many chances left, and it was likely down to them if the shark was to die.

Captain Krauser hefted the shell in, at last, as Spahn tried to make the last few desperate adjustments. Shutting the chamber with a clank, his eyes fell on the body of Dr Arnold, and his heart sank. The doctor had been a good man, and it was a shame that he had ended up this way.

"Hertz shot him." shouted Spahn from the firing seat. "The poor doctor flipped his lid when he saw the shark, and, well, I guess that old Hertz just wasn't in the mood for it. Shot him right there on the deck."

"Goddamn it, Hertz," muttered the captain. "I just thought I was starting to see the hero in him."

Spahn laughed. "None of us are heroes, Captain. We blow up merchants and sailors and then we run and hide. Does that sound like heroism?"

Krauser said nothing. The shark was on them.

***

Kleiner grabbed two of the men working in the torpedo bay and chivvied them along, helping and bullying them into sliding the twenty foot long torpedo into its tube. Even with the pulleys, chains and belts there to make the load easier to manage, it was backbreaking work, and they all knew that time was against them.

Just as things seemed to be moving smoothly, several torpedoes broke loose, rolling across the floor in a chaotic flurry. One of the men was crushed and lay under its weight, screaming for help. Water sprayed in through the holes the shark's teeth had ground and sliced through the U-616's hull.

Finally, they pushed a G7a steam torpedo home, and closed the bulkhead. Spinning the bulkhead closed, Kleiner muttered a silent prayer, and gave the order to fire.

***

Krauser and Spahn both shouted in terror as the megalodon crashed its jaws down around the prow of the boat. The cleaver-like teeth sank deep into the hull, buckling and cracking the black metal of the U-616 as if it were cheap plastic. The colossal shark grunted out a belch of fetid air, and Spahn fainted dead away.

Krauser was the last man up on deck, and he was alone with the Shark of the North Sea.

Pure adrenaline fuelling his movements once more, he clambered into the firing chair, and made the final adjustments to the deck gun's trajectory and aiming reticle. Thinking of his wife and baby, he muttered a final prayer before beginning the firing sequence.

-EIGHTEEN-

The White Ghost ground down its teeth as hard as it could against the hard metal of the submarine. This hunt had gone on for long enough, now – far, far too long. It was injured, and it was hungry and it was tired. It could feel the screaming of the men inside, and knew that the time had come. Still holding the submarine in its jaws, it kicked down hard with its tail and ploughed the submarine underwater, dragging it down to the depths.

Krauser was just centimetres from hitting the firing button when he found himself thrown onto the deck, and then – with a cacophonous splash – he was suddenly underwater. It took him a moment to realise what had happened. Satisfied that it had weakened the submarine enough, the White Ghost had grabbed the entire submarine side on in its jaws, and dragged them down into the depths to drown. Krauser's lungs rapidly filled with water, having had no time to prepare himself, and he instinctively kicked up and away from the boat, towards the surface. He was desperate to take one last breath before he returned to finish the battle with the monster that had destroyed his submarine, killed his compatriots and terrorised these waters for far too long.

At last he broke the surface and gasped for breath, sweeping the salt water from his eyes. Looking around, all that he could see of the U-616 was a foamy wake, ringed by small pieces of debris that he could barely recognise: part of a strut, a plank of wood from the deck, a tattered piece of uniform.

He screamed in frustration and insolent rage, knowing there was nothing he could do.

He had failed his crew.

***

Kleiner was now up to his armpits in water, and the torpedo bay was filling fast. The shark was shaking the boat from side to side once again. Kleiner quickly learnt that maintaining his footing was almost impossible. He reached desperately for the torpedo firing switch, and was thrown back, falling hard and cracking his tailbone. He swallowed water before managing to stumble to his feet, and reach for the switch once more.

He spared a thought for his family, and all the friends he had lost – and would lose that day – and fired the torpedo.

The G7a steam driven torpedo travelled a distance of six inches before colliding with the hard palette of the roof of the shark's mouth, and exploded with a warhead comparable to three hundred kilograms of TNT.

The shark never knew what hit it, and nor did Kleiner, or any of the remaining crew of the U-616.

***

Krauser was catapulted almost fifty metres through the air by the force of the explosion. He felt the air around him turning hot and dry, singeing his hair and toasting his skin. When at last he hit the water again, it felt like a solid wall, knocking all the breath from his lungs. He swallowed a deep gulp in shock, before managing to right himself and kick back up to the surface, spluttering for breath. He thought he was going to pass out, but knew that if he did he was as good as dead. He lay floating on his back for a while, trying to muster the energy to right himself and decide what to do next.

He felt the impact of debris and shark meat peppering the water around him, and knew that at long last, the battle was finally over. He didn't know exactly what had happened; he could only hazard vague guesses. All that was certain was that his submarine was gone, and so was his White Ghost.

After what seemed like hours, he finally managed to muster enough energy to right himself, and so he did.

About a hundred metres away, the ocean was on fire, as some fluke of the explosion must have cast diesel fuel to the surface. The ocean was a vile, dark purple as the salt water had mixed with engine oil and the blood of the shark - and also of his crewmates, no doubt. A tattered skull and crossbones pennant floated past him, and he grabbed it and stuck it in his pocket without really knowing why.

He screamed suddenly, startled almost out of his skin by the blast of a ship's horn. Turning in the water, he saw a fishing vessel of some kind. It must have been the vessel he had glimpsed briefly on the horizon what seemed like hours ago. It was a nondescript, battered ship, and he had no clue as to its nationality. It was backlit by the sun, and he thought for a moment that he had died aboard a boat, and that this was how a sailor would see heaven. That seemed plausible, didn't it?

Eventually he heard voices, and the sound was familiar, though not a language he understood; Dutch or Norwegian, perhaps. He felt his eyes fluttering and he rose and fell in the twilight between sleep and wake.

Eventually the boat came alongside, and he felt strong arms reaching down for him.

***

The first thing he heard was a familiar Norwegian accented German.

"It looks like you have had an even worse time of it than I had, August."

Krauser opened his eyes with a snap, gasping with delight at the sight of Arild Dahlen. The Norwegian sailor was alive, dry, and wearing what was obviously one of the fisherman's spare clothes. Looking down he saw that he was wearing a similar thick, roll-necked sweater and black trousers. He looked up and around, seeing that he was in a two-man cabin, occupying the lower bunk. His tattered and singed clothes were hung up upon a line to dry. He blinked away the sleep and tried to ignore his pounding headache, not to mention the dull pain from the bullet wound in his arm. "Jesus, Dahlen, how long was I out for?"

"You were partially conscious when the men here brought you aboard. You then slept for…nearly forty eight hours now. It sounds like you had a hell of a day."

"I guess so. It's coming back slowly."

"The boat is Norwegian. My countrymen here picked me up purely by chance, floating in the water. They were just turning back for home when we heard the explosion. I managed to convince them to turn back, and take a look in case there were any survivors. I knew it had to be the U-616."

"You were heading for home? Didn't you think to help us out? You knew we were still being attacked by that thing!"

Dahlen sighed. "I did not tell the men here about the shark. I just told them I had fallen overboard and my ship had not found me. I did not want to get them involved. Truth be told, August, I had had enough. I saw my chance to get away from the shark, and get home. The fact the shark was distracted by the U-616 was an opportunity that I exploited."

"You left us!"

"Yes. Yes, I did."

"Fine actions from the man who told us that I was wrong for – what was it? For leaving those sailors as a distraction! As bait! As *chum*!"

"I understand your decision now."

"You accused us of being so 'divorced from your humanity' and then you treat us exactly the same! The crew of the U-616 were men, not some terrain to be taken advantage of!"

"Please, August. Please. I apologised for my words some time ago. I understand now why you did what you did. I have learned that I am no hero."

Krauser slumped back onto the bed, massaging his eyes with the balls of his hands. "None of us are heroes, Arild."

Dahlen offered Krauser a cigarette, which he accepted gratefully. Eventually the captain asked; "Were there any other survivors?"

Dahlen shook his head, sadly. "None. We found some pieces; but no, you were the only one alive."

"And the shark?"

"It was one hell of an explosion."

Krauser nodded. "I guess they finally found a torpedo that wasn't a dud."

Dahlen smiled, ruefully. "We're on our way back to Norway."

"Where I'm to remain a prisoner of war, I suppose?"

"No, actually. The fishermen and I will arrange for you to 'fall' into German hands. We both know that you have a rather pressing engagement you need to make it home for. It is the least I can do for you – and, of course, Mrs Krauser."

Krauser smiled. "Thank you. What will you do?"

Dahlen shrugged. "I will hang around the docks. Beer. Women. Another ship will come in, and I will sign on. There is always a need for crew, and there will be all the time that your Kriegsmarine are sinking ships."

The men fell silent for several minutes, each thinking over the excitement, terror and – yes – even the good fortune of the past few days. Eventually, it was Dahlen that broke the silence. "Do you think it is dead?"

"Yes."

"You are so sure?"

Krauser stubbed his cigarette out and exhaled a lungful of smoke. "If it were still alive, it would have hunted me. It would still be hunting me now. It would have attacked this ship. No, my friend, it is dead. It lies at the bottom of the ocean with the other dark, dead things. With the other ghosts."

Dahlen shivered and lit another cigarette. "What if it is following this ship?"

Krauser sat up sharply, propping himself on his elbows. "Why? What have you seen?"

"I have seen nothing; I have heard nothing. It is just...I do not know."

"Arild…when this war is over, I want you to come find me in Berlin. I'd like us to remain friends. I want you to meet my wife – and my son or daughter, when they are born."

"I would like that very much, August. And, if there is not a Berlin, you can find me in Oslo."

They smiled, and then were silent. Krauser was just drifting off to sleep again, when Dahlen's deadpan voice interrupted him. "What do you think it was?"

"It was hungry. Is that not all that was important?"

Dahlen chuckled. "Not a sea monster? Not a dinosaur? Not the devil himself?"

Krauser yawned, and lay down. "It was a shark. A big one, mind, but still just a shark. Anything else would…raise too many questions."

"Just a shark?"

"Just a shark."

The friends fell asleep, as the ship carried them towards Norway, and whatever awaited them next.